I0577974

DEAD COLD

JANE HEAFIELD

Copyright © 2020 Jane Heafield
The right of Jane Heafield to be identified as the Author of the Work has been
asserted by her in accordance to the Copyright, Designs and Patents Act 1988.
First published in 2020 by Bloodhound Books
Apart from any use permitted under UK copyright law, this publication may
only be reproduced, stored, or transmitted, in any form, or by any means, with
prior permission in writing of the publisher or, in the case of reprographic
production, in accordance with the terms of licences issued by the Copyright
Licensing Agency.
All characters in this publication are fictitious and any resemblance to real
persons, living or dead, is purely coincidental.
www.bloodhoundbooks.com

Print ISBN 978-1-913419-83-7

PART I

1

---

*M*urder makes it so interesting. *It's like getting a wrapped present: you never know what's inside. Sometimes it's bad, but sometimes you get exactly what you want. Murder is the same. The bad ones are the bloated bodies pulled from lakes, or rotten, stinking corpses found in the woods, and I collect those as you might collect festive socks. But every now and then the other kind comes along. Merry Christmas to me. A fresh kill amongst the masses.*

The scene was picture-perfect when she arrived, bathed in the swirling palette of twilight, like a movie shot. The residents of this bland street were at windows, in gardens, on the street, some dressed for work, others in pyjamas. Added to the mass of bodies were uniformed police officers protecting an inner cordon around the front gate and garden of the death house. Every face she saw was loaded with shock, or fear. It was beautiful. Perfect.

Murder usually happens elsewhere in the world, not on normal people's doorsteps, and it happens to faceless nobodies they've never met. People don't want murder in their faces. It terrifies them, the stark reality of it, knowing it can happen anywhere, not only on TV. When I arrive at a murder scene, they watch me with awe, because I am a superhero who tackles the terrifying reality of murder head-on. I do not hide away from killers. I hunt them down.

The street was clogged with emergency vehicles and barred at both ends by police cars. No forensics vehicles here yet, and none of her team's cars. Good: the limelight was hers for the time being. One of the police cars slid back to give her access and police tape strung across the street slid up and over her windscreen as she rolled into the cordon. Gawkers looked away from the death house to watch her approach, aware that someone important had arrived.

She checked her appearance in the sun visor's mirror, wiping away a tint of remaining lipstick she'd missed when removing her makeup before she drove here. Myriad eyes were on her as she stepped out of the vehicle, her exit nimble, graceful, and today the door didn't whack her shoulder as it shut.

Typically, she would stand here a few seconds to soak up the moment, but not this morning. Memories of last night put shame and guilt in her heart. At a dinner party, one of her sister's obnoxious friends had been drunk and had asked her: how can you deal with death all the time? Doesn't it rot your soul? Annoyed by the assumption, and loose-tongued by alcohol, she'd launched into a spiel that had embarrassed everyone: *Murder makes it so interesting...*

'Are you the with the investigating team?' said a fifty-something uniformed officer who approached. He reminded her of Dan, although he was at least fifteen years older than her husband. She immediately didn't like him for this childish reason. She tapped her ID, on a lanyard hanging down between her breasts.

'Detective Inspector Lizzie Miller, MIT 2 out of Woodseats,' she said, even though he had read her ID. It sounded good to say aloud, especially to uniforms. 'But I go by Liz. You were the responding officer? Where's the Review Team?'

He looked her up and down, then back at her ID. 'No team sent, Ms Miller. Just me and my partner, Ramble. He's inside the house still. I called it in. Definitely murder.'

When a Major Inquiry Team got the call about a body, they sent a couple of detectives – a Review Team – ahead to appraise the scene, to make sure hardcore murder investigators' time wasn't wasted. If the diagnosis is accident or natural causes, local CID detectives got the case. Only on a cry of foul play did MIT's wheels kick into gear.

Here, though, the Review Team had been bypassed. On the word of a bobby. Strange.

She again looked at the cars on the street. Bates might have used a different vehicle... but hers was the only civilian one within the cordon. 'No other detectives have arrived? You've not heard from a DCI Bates? The senior investigating officer?'

'Not yet, ma'am. Nor the scene-of-crime people. You're the first. I'm Hitchfield.'

Her chief inspector was usually the first officer on scene once they'd had confirmation they were dealing with a murder. If he was late, something was wrong. Her mobile was in the car, but she made a firm decision right then not to go fetch it.

'What time did you arrive, Hitchfield?'

'Six thirteen, ma'am.'

'What time did you call it in as "definitely murder"?'

'Six eighteen.'

Thirty-four minutes ago. DCI Bates had called her twenty-seven minutes ago. Bates lived a little closer to the scene, about fifteen minutes' drive as opposed to her twenty, but perhaps he'd gone early-morning fishing again. Quite conceivable that distance and traffic meant he was still en route.

'What happened to get you sent here, Hitchfield?'

'There was a 999 call from someone claiming to be a neighbour, who said we should "check out" 88 Pond Street because the owners might be in trouble. I was told to respond here and check the occupants were okay. They're not.'

Hitchfield gave a sly point at an old woman standing in the wooden porch of the semi attached to the death house, arms folded as if she knew she was important and was awaiting attention.

'When we arrived, the old lady approached and told me that at about three thirty in the morning she heard a noise out back of the houses. She went to her back-bedroom window and saw a black shape in the neighbours' garden. But that was all she'd said. Anything further she would only give to a detective. She was specific. Detective only. Maybe she thinks Inspector Morse is coming down.'

On another day, buoyed by the perfect scene, she might have laughed at his joke. But Bates's absence was worrying her. 'Is the old lady the one who made the 999 call, because of this intruder she saw?'

'I asked. But she'll only talk to detectives. I didn't push.'

'Just so I'm clear. The call to police came at somewhere around 6am, but the witness over there says she saw an intruder at three thirty?'

'I know: why the gap? But she won't talk to me.'

'And then you went inside?'

'Yes.' Hitchfield and his partner, Ramble, who was still in the house, had knocked on the locked front and back doors, but gotten no answer. They'd peered in the kitchen window, but seen nothing out of place. Back at the front of the property, unable to see inside and fearing a threat to life, they'd booted in the door. And found two people dead in the kitchen, a man and a woman. Ramble was still inside, guarding the front door in case anyone got past Hitchfield.

While he relayed this tale, Liz scanned the street. Two rows of semi-detached two-storey buildings, set behind neat lawns and driveways, with bay windows and front doors shielded by tiny porches. Somewhere between middle and lower class, given the mix of commercial and trade vehicles. A fair bunch of for-sale signs about, which she always thought was a bad signal.

Hitchfield finished by declaring he'd cordoned off the house, blocked the road and called it in. All the right procedures: she decided she liked this guy now, despite the resemblance to her husband.

Liz walked over to the neighbour's garden hedge. The old lady approached. She had the sort of face that, many years ago, would have turned heads. 'You a detective? I only want to tell detectives. Not these woodentops.'

There was a term Liz hadn't heard for ages. 'I'm a detective. Inspector Liz Miller. Do not talk to anyone but me, okay? Others will come, but I want you to deal only with me, okay?'

The old lady nodded. 'Are the Lawlers dead?'

Liz ignored the question. 'I'll come for your statement soon. Talk only to me, please.' She headed back to Hitchfield.

He said, 'I heard her say the name Lawler. Some of these gawkers shouted it. I checked the electoral register on my mobile and Mark and Vicky Lawler live here. No kids. The old lady says they were away on holiday and weren't due back until later today. Must have come back early. Maybe a burglar thought they'd still be out.'

Unwilling to be drawn into theory with a uniform, and eager to see the crime scene, she approached the driveway gate of the death house. The gate was manned by another officer and a third stood at the front door. The crime tape across the gate and front door made her again think of this murder scene as a present to her. A brick box, with goodies inside. If they'd known what drove her, the police might well have tied the tape in a bow across the front porch.

Both officers lifted the tape to allow her through, as if she were royalty. She couldn't help a glance back at the growing crowd, to see what they made of this. Hitchfield was right behind her. In the porch, which was barely big enough for them both, they dragged on plastic shoe covers and latex gloves and stepped inside. Liz had a full-body protective suit in her car, but something about Bates's absence urged her to get inside the house quickly... before it was too late.

The other officer, Ramble, was standing in the hallway, reading notes and letters pinned on a corkboard behind the front door. Hitchfield shut the door behind them. Ramble promised he'd been careful where he stepped and had touched nothing. He looked her up and down, head to toe and back again, but tried to hide his inspection.

A short wooden-floored hallway led to a closed door at the end, with other doors in the walls. Beside the front door was a portrait of a man and a woman in marriage gear, standing by a white vintage car, a church in the background. She recognised the church as the one she'd passed on her way here, located at the edge of the estate. An inset showed a close-up of the happy couple's faces. They were a handsome pair, early thirties in the photograph. Grinning, loving life. Not anymore.

The portrait hung above a small table scattered with mail. Without touching the letters, Liz leaned close and saw the addressees were Mark and Victoria Lawler. Sadly, one of the letters was from a life insurance company. It reminded her she needed to remove a beneficiary from her own policy.

The tranquil nature of the scene evaporated close to the kitchen door. Here, red smears in the rough shape of feet, heading away from the kitchen. Good old-fashioned bloody shoeprints.

2

The bloody shoeprints ended partway down the hall, as if whoever had made them had taken flight like Superman.

She also saw blood on the left wall, right where the prints ended. A smear in a sort of sideways, ragged love-heart shape, surrounded by spatter. Closer, she realised the heart shape was a pair of shoe impressions, with the heels overlapped and the front of the outsoles leaning away from each other. She was reminded of childhood white winters, smacking her footwear against a wall to clean them. Here, though, someone had tried to dislodge excess blood, not snow.

While taking close-up photographs of the smears with her camera phone, she spotted something white stuck in the blood. She used a pair of tweezers to remove it. It appeared to be a tiny fragment of paper. There was no blood on it except where it had stuck to the wall.

This enriched her hypothesis that the scrap had been caught in the tread of a shoe, only one side exposed, and had dislodged when the sole was slammed against the wall. She dropped the miniscule piece into a small evidence bag.

Neither policeman asked what she'd found, nor questioned why she hadn't left it for the forensic scientists. She knew why: more disturbing things lay in the kitchen.

As she approached the kitchen, it was slowly revealed to her beyond the doorway. First, a long worktop with sink, cooker, microwave and a window into the back garden. Then, further left, she saw a tall fridge-freezer standing in the middle of the room, in front of the washing machine and angled towards her. Brand new, given the blue tape sealing the doors closed and an energy efficiency label on the front.

Blood spatter was across virtually the whole floor, but a trail of it thickened as it disappeared behind the freezer. Bloody foot-prints led towards and past her, out into the hallway.

'No one come in.' Avoiding the bigger spatters of blood, she stepped towards the freezer, so she could see the space in the wall units where the item would sit. And what was there instead.

Two bodies. Dressed and sitting side by side, jammed between the dishwasher and washing machine. Their smashed heads were tilted back, which emphasised great rents below their chins where their throats used to be. Their faces were more gone than not. Vented blood had soaked and crusted their cloth-ing, painted the floor beneath them, and coated the sides of the white goods. Only a future homebuyer with no knowledge would ever again see this place as tranquil, if morbid curiosity didn't force the council to erase the entire building from existence.

Liz stared at the bodies and tried to dampen her relief. Not a case of murder-suicide, as she'd feared. Murder-suicide meant a killer already known and already out of the game. All that remained was to learn the *why*, which only really helped the victims' families. Here, though, she had a whodunnit. There was a killer to hunt. It could only have been sweeter if the bodies had been outside, allowing the crowd to watch her work.

Liz retraced her own steps back into the hallway as she heard at least two cars arrive. But none of the new vehicles had had the throaty growl of her boss's faulty exhaust.

She knew she was about to lose this gift of a case.

3

———

The host of new vehicles included an ambulance. The paramedics jumped out, but Liz gave them a wave that said they could slow down. Realising they weren't vital here, the two men got back in their vehicle to wait.

Two forensics vans. Six people already at the back, donning white plastic suits. They looked and she gave a nod in greeting.

An unmarked car. Two detectives. One, a black female about fifty years of age. The officer with her was much younger and was the sort of handsome DC the TV liked to slot next to grizzled old inspectors for eye candy. And she recognised him: Ralph Hooper, a mouthy little sod who'd worked at another station of hers several years back. Hooper did nothing as she approached, but the black lady raised her warrant card. Detective Sergeant Sienna Todd. She looked puzzled. But Liz had no confusion. DCI Bates still wasn't here.

'I guess I'm off the case,' Liz said.

Todd's puzzlement vanished. 'Oh, you were called first? I did wonder why they gave a Sheffield case to Barnsley. It must be down to your SIO.'

Barnsley was MIT 3. South Yorkshire had four Major Investigation Teams, one for each district. MIT 2 covered Sheffield, and this was Crookes, Sheffield, so it should have been Liz's case. But Barnsley's MIT 3 had been sent. Why? And why so soon after Liz had gotten the call to attend from her boss, DCI Alan Bates? Something to do with Bates, as the woman had said. And not because he was bloody running late.

'I must have missed a call. My phone is in the car.'

'Then you'd better be on your way,' Hooper told her. His attitude surprised his colleague. Liz wanted to warn him to watch his mouth in front of a superior officer, but instead ignored him.

'Oh, okay. So, have you been inside?' DS Todd asked.

'I have. There's two uniformed responders in there right now. The old one's got friends in high places, I suspect. I think he called this in as murder and his word was accepted, so no Review Team was sent. But it was a good call. Two bodies. A lot of blood.'

Liz pointed at the old lady neighbour, still standing on her doorstep with folded arms, waiting for her turn. 'The lady next door said she saw someone around the back early in the morning. She must have called it in, yet there's a gap between when she saw an intruder in the backyard and when the call was made.'

'Okay, thank you, we'll get to her,' Todd said.

Liz jabbed a thumb at the growing crowd behind the crime tape. 'When nosey neighbours see massive police and forensics activity centred on a house, they expect the people living there to exit in handcuffs or body bags. Either the Lawlers were another Fred and Rose West, or they lie dead. What some of these people are going to do is hop on their phones to get answers and spread the gossip. You need to get liaison officers over to the parents now, before they learn the news through Facebook.'

Todd nodded. 'We know what to do. Thank you.'

Hooper wasn't as sweet: 'Our SIO is usually unflappable, but he'll get angry if you're still here when he arrives.'

Liz wanted to laugh right in his face. 'Where is he?'

In answer, another car arrived and was passed through the cordon. A man in a tracksuit under a leather jacket got out. DCI Liam Bennet, she knew. Head of Barnsley's MIT 3. The four top MIT dogs often had meetings together, but, as a DI, she'd never met him. He was a tall guy with tight muscles and a flat-top. Handsome. Early forties, she guessed. He could play a TV detective for sure. The only giveaway he actually was a police officer was the ID lanyard around his neck and a portable fingerprint scanner in his hand.

The crowd was watching and their scrutiny seemed to unnerve him a little, although he turned to the eager faces and took a photo with his phone. He ignored shouted questions and approached the trio of detectives.

Liz saw the same puzzled expression the two other detectives had given her, so she didn't wait for the question. 'My phone was in the car.' She saw understanding cross his face. He put out his hand to shake, which she did. And he gave the ID round her neck only a brief glance.

'Better go call your super, DI Miller.'

She didn't move. 'Did this one get shifted to MIT 3 because something's happened to DCI Bates? No one has told me anything.'

'Your superintendent will. You should call him.'

'Will do. I should mention that the old lady over there at number 86 said she won't talk to anyone but me. She gave no reason why. I didn't influence her. I'll be around for a few minutes if you need me to chat to her.'

'We don't,' Hooper said.

Liz rushed to her car, found her phone and, as predicted, it displayed a missed call from her super. Two, in fact. Unable to get an answer, he'd followed with a text.

BATES INJURED IN CAR CRASH EN ROUTE. HE'S OKAY. BARNS-LEY'S GOT THIS ONE. HEAD ON BACK.

With the lead detective of Sheffield's murder squad out through injury, the head of her station, Superintendent Roy Allenberg, would have informed his own boss, the District Commander for Sheffield. The commander would have kicked the case to his colleague in Barnsley, who had then sent his own detective team. Nothing she could do about this. They were all South Yorkshire police and no argument about jurisdiction would help.

She didn't want to call her super back yet. Instead, she removed the plastic evidence bag from her pocket. With two pairs of tweezers, she extracted the tiny scrap of paper and spread it open. It was the size of her thumbnail.

Printed on it was a black curve of ink like a right-hand bracket and, to its right, a straight diagonal line. Like two slashes, one curved. The paper was torn, suggesting the ink was part of a bigger picture, maybe a portion of large-print text. Both were on a pink background.

She tried to give this piece of evidence her full attention, but her gaze was apprehended by the detectives and the forensics team. They were preparing to enter the death house via a tent that had been rapidly erected over the front porch.

She stamped on the footbrake, feeling like a teenager who'd been excluded from a New Year's Eve party. It particularly burned that the crowd was engrossed by the main players. Liz was nobody's focus. Even when Bennet and DS Todd vanished into the house, it was Hooper who became a point of fascination as he spoke with a uniformed officer.

This clue. She had to work it. It could be the key. As she studied the scrap, she wondered if the curves on ink could be numbers? The straight could be a seven, and the curve part of a nine. Ninety-seven.

Then she had it. She dialled another number. When her station's switchboard operator answered, she gave her name and asked to be put through to a department.

'The café?' The operator sounded unsure, as if she must have heard wrong.

She hadn't. Liz repeated her request and the next voice she heard was a male who introduced himself as the café manager. Liz again gave her name and rank and asked if Betty Jones was in today. She was, she was due on salad prepping, but wasn't on shift for another half hour or so. A doctor's appointment for her ankle. 'Anything I can help with?'

'I want you to get Betty to call me when she comes in. As soon as, please.'

The café man said something else, but Liz cut him off with a goodbye and hung up the phone as her rear-view showed another car being let through the cordon. Not a police car or one belonging to her team. Based on the distinguished face she saw behind the wheel, she figured this was the Home Office pathologist. Annoyingly, his vehicle got a lot of consideration as it found a clear piece of kerb near the death house. You didn't get TV detective fiction without one of these men or women at a crime scene, bent over a corpse.

And watching it all was the old lady at her garden gate. 'Don't let me down,' Liz mouthed her way. Her attention returned to the house, as she wondered what glorious clues were in there, awaiting DCI Bennet.

4

____

An old boss had once set a ten-minute alarm at a crime scene. Intrigued, Bennet had watched him stroll round a dead woman's house, getting to know her. Only upon the ding did his boss head for his first look at the body. Already somewhat acquainted with her, it had enhanced his boss's sense of injustice and kicked him up a gear. It was a habit Bennet had adopted. He would visit the kitchen last.

First, the living room. Plain, a little untidy, too colourful. A giant bookcase spread across the whole of one wall, featuring romcom, supernatural and fantasy novels and DVDS. A single shelf, at the top, was dedicated to sports videos and publications. There was an Xbox 360 by the TV and a gaming chair nearby, an empty lager can in the cup holder. An armchair had a drawing pad and a fiction book on one arm and overlapping teacup rings on the other.

In a cupboard under the stairs, he found cleaning gear and a hook-rack with summer jackets rendered useless by the December chill. A wicker basket contained a jagged mass of coat hangers. A high shelf bore a clutter of tools. The slanted ceiling had been half painted and abandoned.

He headed upstairs. In the front room, bedside cabinets gave a clear indication of who slept on which side of the bed. The built-in wardrobe had female clothing hanging from a rail and male items folded on a shelf above. A laundry bag had overflowed. On each side of the bed, protruding from beneath the mattress, were straps ending in ankle and wrist restraints. Bennet had searched too many homes to be embarrassed or surprised.

The second bedroom seemed to be used for storage, mainly books in clear plastic boxes and clothing in refuse bags, with a space cleared for a small table and laptop. The third contained exercise equipment, although here items had also been stored, suggesting the fitness gear was rarely used.

The house spoke of a couple who had gone beyond the early phases of love and lust and could enjoy their own company together, so to speak. Bennet couldn't recall if he'd ever reached that level of comfort with his ex.

Finally, he entered the bathroom, whose window the offender had used to gain entry. But he avoided the exact point of entry, instead focusing on toiletries placed upon the sill. They had been separated, hers on the left, his on the right, a clear gap of five inches between them. The sink was toothpaste-stained. A cheesy-looking vampire book lay beside the bath, its pages fat and fanned due to soaking.

With a minute remaining on his alarm, Bennet turned his attention to the point of entry. The casement window was shut, but the handle was turned wide. There was a cable restrictor, designed for preventing children or the elderly from hurting themselves, but here, in a house occupied by two able-minded adults, its role was crime prevention. Fat lot of good it had done. The wire bundle and plastic sheathing were designed to be tough to cut, but here it had been burned through.

His alarm dinged.

As he was walking down the stairs, the front door opened and a middle-aged man in a suit under his plastic examiner coveralls entered with a bag. Not a face Bennet recalled, but he knew this was the Home Office pathologist. The chap didn't look happy.

Perhaps hearing the pathologist's entry, DS Todd and DC Hooper entered from the kitchen. They introduced themselves. The older man was Home Office Forensic Pathologist Dr Jacob Huntley MB, ChB, BMSc (Hons), FRCPath, MFFLM.

'Two bodies, I hear,' he said in a West Country accent. 'Twice the work.'

'Yes. It's a couple we think are Mark–'

'No, no.' The pathologist raised a hand like a traffic warden. 'Do not tell me. Victimology is your domain, but I don't require knowing about the dead. No hardened fact or speculative conjecture, not in the arena of scientific analysis.'

It had sounded like a telling off, but the pathologist had a smile. Bennet wasn't sure if it was a joke. 'Excuse me?'

'If I hear the victim is a skateboarder, perhaps I'll attribute a knee scrape to that pastime, which will effect a clouded overview. No details, please. Not even names.'

It was no joke. 'A first for my ears. Most pathologists want to know as much as possible. They think it helps.'

'It's a cloudy sky in their world, I imagine. No details. I will do my work, present my case. This was meant to be my day off, you know?'

He was getting a fat fee, so what was the problem? He took out his phone. 'What's your mobile number?'

'Ah, the interim report. Your Golden Hour. The bane of my life. *Please make an early guess while the scalpel is still in your hand,* eh? I recall the Jainist parable of the blind men and an elephant.'

'Are you suggesting I hold off investigating this until you've finished the entire autopsy? This one is a force priority. I'd like at least one of the autopsies completed by morning end. Both today.'

The pathologist paused. Was he actually considering Bennet's question?

'Mr Huntley, there's a killer loose out there and I don't want to give him half a day's head start. So let's go look at Mark and Vicky Lawler and see what you can tell me. If you're fast, you can get home and still have some of your day off.'

5

———

Done with talking to police officers, the young male detective, Hooper, approached the old lady at her garden gate. Watching, Liz held her breath as they talked. The old lady shook her head and pointed at Liz's car. And when Hooper gave Liz's vehicle a murderous look, she thanked her lucky stars.

Hooper pulled out his phone and made a call. Soon after, Bennet exited the death house and spoke to his DC. Another finger pointed at her car, and this time the tall DCI threw a burning glare her way. When he approached, she put her phone to her ear and pretended to be on a call. Bennet's rap on her window even got him a raised finger – wait a moment – as she continued the pantomime.

When she put the phone away, she buzzed down her window.

'DCI Bennet, what can I do for you?'

'Inspector Miller, I seem to have a possible witness who won't speak to my team, as you said. But the lady claims you told her not to.'

The silly old bag. Liz considered a lie: I only meant don't talk to the media. 'I apologise. I'm good with witnesses and I wanted first read on her. But when I told her, this case was still mine.'

He didn't look convinced, and soon proved it: 'DCI Bates is a drinking pal of mine and we get loose-tongued at the pub. I'm sure he's told you a few stories about some of my team. And I once heard about his inspector, who enjoys being centre stage in high-profile cases. I expected you to try to dig your heels in. But you really need to head on back to your station.'

Bates had been gossiping about her? She was disheartened. 'Well, it's a bit unfair of my boss to say. But he's wrong. I'm not trying to infiltrate. I want to help a little before I go back. I had a look at the victims' social media. Their Facebook pages are exploding with comments. There are friends asking if they're okay and why all the police are outside his house. I think some might be heading over here. Could help to get officers to the family before others beat them to it.'

'This one is already hitting the news. I know the process, DI Miller, so I really must insist now. Leave my crime scene.'

She got out of her car. He was forced to step back as her door opened. 'DCI Bennet, I apologise. I'll go explain to the lady. I'll tell her my people are no longer involved. Or, since she's willing to talk to me, I could go in there and ask her some questions. I'll pass right on whatever she tells me. And then I'll get lost.'

It was a major punt, barely worth the effort involved in voicing the words, and when her gall elicited a disbelieving shake of the head, she half-expected him to have her escorted away. Thus, it was a curveball when he said, 'Interview the lady and record it if she doesn't mind. Pass what you get on to my constable, Hooper. Then, please, get lost.'

She could have kissed him.

6

The old lady told her to call her May. 'You seem young and sweet for a detective. Why would you do such a stressy job?'

Like May, many people were surprised that Liz was a detective inspector, probably because TV had convinced them all sleuths were grizzled old men. Liz was used to people taking a long look at her ID, as if expecting to see it stamped with 'Trainee'. May's question, in various forms, was one Liz had endured so often that she'd formulated a standard, vague answer. 'Criminals took my parents away and I swore revenge.'

'Oh my God. That's horrible. What happened?'

'Why don't you tell me what you saw, May?'

They were in her cramped living room. It was homely, with far too many cushions and ornaments. But a comfortable niche, Liz understood. May was in a long skirt made of a thick grey material Liz thought should itch like mad, and a blouse that was far too see-through. She stood by the window, staring out at the activity in the street. She struck Liz as a busybody who liked to know everything that went on in her neighbourhood. She had probably agreed to answer questions more out of curiosity than a desire to help.

May paused, as if considering pushing her earlier question about Liz's parents. But a busybody's mind had a healthy appetite. 'Are the Lawlers dead?'

'I can't talk about what's going on, you understand?'

'Did a robber think they'd still be out?'

'The holiday you mentioned. They were due back today, you said?'

'They went to the Canary Islands, didn't they? With their National Lottery winnings.'

Intriguing. 'How much did they win? And when did they go?'

'Oooh, they went last week. They won a few thousand pounds two weeks ago, enough for a holiday. Mind you, Mark should have used it on his fine. They went to the Canary Islands, where they had that plane crash all those years ago. They were supposed to be back later today, but obviously they came back early and disturbed a burglar. So, they're dead, aren't they?'

'I can't talk about what's happened, May. What fine are you talking about?'

'Mark. He was arrested, wasn't he?'

Liz perked up. 'I don't know. For what?'

'Taxi driving. But he's not a taxi driver. He lost his licence and got a fine, so they had to sell their car. I'm sure you'll see this on your files somewhere.'

Liz could have groaned. If Mark Lawler had a criminal conviction for drugs or gang activity or rape or something else meaty, it could have provided motive and suspects. 'I'm sure we will, May. But back to what happened. You called the police? Because of this intruder you saw?'

'You wouldn't have those forensical people in white suits if they weren't dead. Have they been murdered?'

'May, we got the call only about an hour ago. There is a gap of two-and-a-half hours between when you saw the intruder and when the call to the police was made.'

'Call? It wasn't me. I didn't call the police.'

That was intriguing. Liz would have to find out more about this phone call to the police. She had assumed it was this old lady, because of the intruder, but her denial left a question mark. 'Tell me about this intruder you spotted last night.'

May turned away from the window and took a seat. About half three this morning, she explained, she couldn't sleep and heard a noise, and looked out to see a man in black at the bottom of the garden. He scaled the wall and was gone.

'You're sure it was a person you saw?'

'You think I'm old and infirm?' May said, not in anger. 'I have it on camera, for your information. What do you say to that? Security for the back, because cars sometimes get vandalised. Mine is there. So, I have it on camera, just in case you think I saw a cat. Oh, there are nine or ten of us on this street with cameras, if you plan to look at them. There's Mrs Ford at 41, but watch out for her dog. The Blackwells at 51 have–'

'We'll get to them, don't worry. Please, May, can I see your CCTV recordings?'

The CCTV set-up was in May's bedroom, whose double bed was half taken up with scattered paperwork that looked like it had been there some time. The half where a husband would sleep, had there been one. She didn't want to ask.

The footage showed May's backyard and one either side. Behind the back fence was a brick wall and beyond that a street. The image was poorly lit. The back gardens were too dark and beyond the grainy street was nothing but a wall of black, as if the earth ended and gave into the gloom of deep space.

With the bad quality of the video factored in, there was no hope of identifying any of the three parked vehicles she could see, if she later found one to be missing. Facial recognition, if a face appeared, would be impossible. How many times had Liz cursed cheap CCTV?

May used a rollerball to position a giant screen pointer over a list of recording files split into hours of the day, then fast-forwarded to the position required. It took her three minutes to do a job that should have taken thirty seconds. Liz had to bite down the urge to grab the rollerball off the old lady.

The video showed a black shape moving down the rear garden on the right, the Lawlers', away from the house. Liz felt a little spurt of joy, but it was short-lived. The form was little more than a moving piece of the night. They'd never get an identification, even if the figure turned and peered at the camera. By the time the shape had reached the back gate, it was little more than a shimmering blob. It slipped through the gateway, then over the wall and onto the street, which would give it an exit either way. The timestamp said 0322.

'So you saw this intruder late last night but didn't phone the police?'

'But there was nothing in his hands, was there? He didn't steal anything. I thought maybe he'd tried the Lawlers' back door and then gave up when it was locked. My God, he killed them, didn't he? And I did nothing.'

The old lady was upset at the idea her reticence might have allowed a murderer to escape. Liz leaned forward and took her gnarly, cold hand. 'May, nobody is saying you did anything wrong or anything is your fault. We don't know what's happened yet, and we don't know if this intruder is involved. And you're right: the intruder wasn't stealing, and he was leaving the area. He would have been long gone by the time the police arrived. It's okay.'

May was going to tell this tale a bunch more times, to detectives who might be less understanding. Not a priority for Liz. 'We'll need this tape.'

'Oh, you mean so you can look back and see when the man in black arrived? I already checked, did it last night. He's not on it. I went all the way back to before it got dark. I think he must have used the front door. Mark and Vicky hide a key in a plant pot on the front porch. I should have told those police who first arrived, but I neglected to. They wouldn't have had to break the door down.'

Liz remembered seeing the plant pot. That needed checking out. 'I need to see for myself.' She cycled back the recording. The black shape zoomed into the house in reverse, but afterwards the only movement was the timestamp counting backwards at speed, and the darkness rapidly sluicing from the sky, until it was blue. Daytime didn't help the video quality though: the deep space beyond the street behind the rear yards had become an impenetrable burning white desert.

Liz slammed the play button when a shape darted into May's backyard, at a quarter past midday. But it was only May herself. She peeked over the fence separating 88 and 86 and seemed to be staring at the death house.

'Oh, that was when the delivery chap was here,' May explained, rather sheepishly. 'I was... well, I was being nosey, trying to see him in their kitchen.'

Liz made a mental note: brand-new freezer, delivered sometime around midday yesterday. She had to dampen the urge to go find this delivery man right now. It was doubtful he was the culprit. But if he wasn't, at least the freezer delivery meant the Lawlers had been killed some time after midday yesterday.

It was good info, but not a clue. Not something she could run with right now. She felt a sense of urgency. 'I'd like to see your back garden, please.'

May nodded. 'You'll have to give me a hand with the door. My son installed these fat hinges and it jams in the frame. Come on.'

The door wasn't too bad. Liz told the old lady to remain behind and walked down the weedy path to the gate. The gate was worse than the back door and Liz nearly ripped off a fingernail trying to scrape it open across the ground. The wall was ahead of her. Between wood and brick was an alleyway running away left and right, along the back gardens.

She stepped into the littered alleyway and stood on tiptoe to peek over the wall. The street beyond was pitted, unkempt, as if unused. And the reason for this became clear as she saw what she'd been unable to on Old Lady May's video. It made her heart sink. Not quite the desolation of deep space, but just as bad from an investigative perspective.

Beyond a chain-link fence running the length of the far side of the street was a shrubbery-infested waste ground. Perhaps it had once been another housing estate, or was going to be, which might explain the presence of this forlorn street.

She clambered ungracefully over the wall and broke a heel when she dropped to the road. There was no pavement, just a border of weeds between tarmac and wall. The three cars she'd seen on video were still present, so unlikely to be a killer's getaway vehicle. They would all face analysis, but right now she was focused only on the chain-link fence.

She crossed the road. What she'd spotted from behind the wall was confirmed with a kick: one corner of a fence panel was loose at the bottom of a post, creating a kind of flap. Wide enough for someone to crawl through. It was a clue, but it sank her heart.

If the killer had used this desolate street to make his exit, his face might have been spotted, and recognised, by someone at a back-bedroom window. Or CCTV throughout the city could track his progress right to a doorstep. But if he had crossed the road and slipped into the vast waste ground, he'd become a shadow in the night. Unseen, and – unless he'd tripped and knocked himself into a coma and still lay out there – long gone.

7

She returned her attention to the scrubland. Thirty metres away was a river, which vanished behind a rise to the right. Beyond, the scrubland continued to the back end of another housing estate a few hundred metres away. To the left and right it turned into rolling fields. If the killer was smart, he would have gone across the open land. The only hope was that he'd gone ahead, into the new estate, and had been captured on camera or seen by witnesses. But either way he was long gone.

Her phone rang. Allenberg. She shouldn't put him off any longer. He would be worried about her lack of communication given that DCI Bates had had a car crash. But she wasn't going to call him right now, out here. Back in the car would be the right time.

She walked on, ungracefully because of the broken shoe heel, and stopped at the edge of the riverbank. The dirty river was fifteen feet wide, six feet below her, no bridge in sight. However, a short way to the right a thick concrete pipe jutted out of one riverbank and burrowed into the other, like an exposed bone in a wound. She stamped a foot on the rusty pipe to test its sturdiness, but made no move to cross. She didn't trust her balancing skills. Fleeing a murder scene in the dead of night, she might have.

Her sense of determination was faltering, the urgency dissipating, and in their place was a growing sense of... loss. She'd hardly suffered a bereavement, but the turmoil inside her felt a little like that. She had hoped to find a jackpot clue, something that would impress her super or DCI Bennet and give them reason to keep her on the Pond Street murder case. But she should have known better. Even the most straightforward murders were no slam-dunk. She had never been likely to solve this one in mere minutes, running around on her own.

So she turned around and headed back. Instead of using Old Lady May's house, she walked along the back road and the side street, which delivered her onto Pond Street. Throughout, she swept her vision back and forth across the ground, seeking clues. A discarded bloodied knife would have been sweet, but she found nothing.

Hooper was outside the death house, reading something on his phone. In his other hand was Bennet's portable fingerprint scanner. She approached him, trying her best to appear casual on her busted shoe.

'Give me your phone.'

He looked annoyed and waved the fingerprint scanner. 'I'm not dawdling around playing solitaire, you know. I'm waiting for the pathologist to finish so I can try to confirm ID. Shouldn't you have left already?'

'The male victim should be on file.' She moved past him, to the porch. There was the plant pot, in a corner by the door. It was an artificial bay laurel ball, but set in real soil. She looked under it and dug her fingers into the dirt and delved into the plastic leaves.

'What are you doing?'

She brushed dirt off her fingers as she returned to Hooper,

and asked for his phone again. She even snapped her fingers. He reluctantly handed it over. She accessed the voice recorder and spoke into it.

'The next-door neighbour, May, has video showing an intruder leaving the crime scene at close to three thirty this morning via the back door. There's no footage of the subject entering the house, suggesting he might have used the front door. Get hold of CCTV from the street and concentrate on around midday. The new freezer was delivered at that time and the delivery man allegedly let himself into the house with a key hidden in a plant pot by the front door. The key has gone. And the neighbour claims she didn't make the emergency call to the police.'

She handed Hooper his phone back. 'How did you get all this information? Not that you should have, you're not even on this case.'

'Someone needs to seize that video.'

'Me. I'm exhibits officer. I know what to do. Some of us know our job and its boundaries.'

The little sod. She knew what he meant. 'Well, part of your job is to keep an entry log, and you never asked me what time I arrived at the scene. Six forty-six.'

She moved past him. The crowd watched her exit the garden and head for her car. She did her best to walk on her toes, look ahead, and ignore a volley of questions. Usually, being under fire like this bloated her ego, but now she felt like a condemned woman being led to the gallows. She quickened her pace. She wished she'd parked right outside the house.

Once beyond the cordon, she glanced back. Most of the crowd was ignoring her. After she was safely cocooned in her vehicle, not a single pair of eyes turned her way. They had seen her for the last time, she knew. Nobody was going to remember her.

8

———————

'Double murder in a house. Doors locked,' Bennet said. 'A married couple called Lawler. Mark and Vicky, both late thirties. We got an anonymous call saying they might be in trouble. Here they are.'

Amongst the forty or so photos Bennet had taken during his look around the house, there were a few of the wall-hung pictures of the dead couple. Bennet chose one of the Lawlers larking around in a passport photo booth. Mark was trying to stick his tongue in his wife's ear, while Vicky had a finger jammed in one of his. At least they'd had smiles immortalised: he'd known of murdered victims who'd left behind no happy photos, and sometimes no photos at all.

But before he could dispatch the image via radio waves, the old man on the other end of the phone said, 'No, no grisly photos. I'm at peace. I'm hunting only carp today. Not murder-suicide, I gather?'

'No. Throats gone, faces smashed up. And a strange scratching on both their left hands.'

'What kind of scratching? Defensive wounds?'

'Doesn't seem so. Not like any I've seen, and not according to the pathologist. There's no other wounds on the arms. It's the backs of both left hands from wrists to knuckles. Bad enough to lacerate the flesh and expose the bones. Strange.'

'So what's your initial thought? Home invasion kill? Quite uncommon. This will be big news. Perp?'

'Gone. A witness says she saw a figure leaving the vicinity of the back of the house around three thirty in the morning, but I'm waiting on more on that. It fits with the pathologist's initial estimate that they were killed about one o'clock. But I pushed him for a quick guesstimate, so it might change.'

Speaking of the pathologist, Bennet saw the man exit the house and head for his car. He ignored the crowd's questions and made a swift getaway. With his in-situ examination complete, the bodies could be transferred to the Medico-Legal Centre for post-mortem.

'Motive?' the old man on the phone asked.

'The Lawlers recently had a lottery win of a few thousand pounds. A neighbour claims they went on holiday and were not due back until later tonight. Holidaymakers can get back at all sorts of late hours, so perhaps they interrupted a burglar. But burglary doesn't sit well in my gut. There was no damage, no drawers or cupboards had been opened.'

'Nothing stolen at all?'

'Their mobile phones are missing. We called the numbers, but they went to voicemail. We'll trace their usage. But until we get family or friends in the house to tell us what's missing, it looks as if the perp took nothing.'

The old fisherman clucked his tongue. 'Perhaps he panicked and fled. He went there to steal, something went wrong, and now there are two bodies. He didn't want to hang around. Maybe he took the phones off the victims as soon as they got home, so they couldn't call for help. You think he might have known about the lottery money? He might be known to the victims.'

'Possibly. It would mean he knew they'd be away. It would mean he had a major problem when he broke in and found them at home and got recognised.'

'Good theory. If he's already got form, he'll go down for a long stretch this time. So he needs a way to keep them quiet. And he picks the worst possible way.'

'There are a few bizarre things though.'

The old fisherman made an excited sound. 'Go on.'

'The bodies were sat side by side in the kitchen, in a slot where the freezer goes. The freezer was brand new, delivered yesterday and not put in place yet. The victims were crammed into that small space, shoulder to shoulder. No sign of a struggle. It doesn't look like the scene of a man panicking upon finding owners in a house he's robbing.'

'He acted calmly, knew what he was doing. You're thinking it seems more like an execution. *They* might have been the target, not money.'

Early into his career, Bennet had learned an important adage: *Find out how a person lived and you'll find out how they died.* Knowing a victim, their personality, history, social circle and so forth, was the springboard from which an investigation launched. It was rare to find no previous association between killer and victim, so getting into their lives was vital. The old man on the phone was asking if there was any evidence the couple was involved in something that might have come back to bite them on the arse.

'So far we know little. We found addresses for family members, so they'll soon be informed. But the first search found no drugs or offensive weapons, no connection to dodgy individuals, no indication other people regularly stay at the house. Neighbours say they were nice people, no enemies.'

'Neighbours don't see behind closed doors. What else was strange?'

'One of the weapons. A smooth blade was used to slit their throats, but the second weapon is the eyebrow-raiser. A house brick, which was used to bash in their faces. A whole brick, given how much brick dust and debris was all over the bodies and around the scene.'

'Is the house undergoing any kind of renovation? Or another on the street?'

Bennet's negative answer made the old man curse softly, and he knew why. A house brick, heavy and cumbersome, was nobody's weapon of choice. Every case he'd ever known involving trauma by rock or brick, the weapon was utilised on the spur of the moment, from the scene. Impulse kill, not premeditated. Killers planning murder didn't carry such an unwieldy weapon, yet this one had.

The old man said, 'The brick might have been breaking-and-entering equipment. He didn't expect to find the victims at home, and had to think on his feet. Maybe he utilised it before he had time to draw his knife.'

'He didn't break in with the brick. There's a busted cable restrictor on the bathroom window. Burned through, it looks like. I've left a message with a robbery expert I know. Hopefully, it's exclusive enough that someone's got form for it. So at first glance it appears that our perp came in by climbing up a drain-pipe. We know that the Lawlers hide a front door key in a plant pot outside the door. That key is gone. The back door is sturdy wood with a night latch, so no key is needed to exit. In through the front and out the back, it appears. We're still looking for fingerprints and DNA. I've ordered samples from the usual important places be fast-tracked. Door handles, taps, etc. And the freezer, of course.'

The old man took time to think. As he did, Bennet saw the

paramedics bring out the first of the bodies on a stretcher. It agitated the crowd.

'It makes no sense to climb a drainpipe with a heavy house brick,' the old man said. 'Maybe that cable restrictor was already cut and is just a red herring. Or the perp cut it to muddy the waters. So, going on the theory that he got in through the front with a key and took it away with him, who knew about the plant pot hiding place?'

'A fair number of the neighbours did. They could have told friends. We're still looking into that. Helpful neighbours of the victims say the freezer was delivered in the early afternoon and the delivery man let himself in, so he probably used that key and put it back. We know the freezer was bought from a local Curry's and that the delivery man is in the warehouse right now. I've got officers on the way to have a chat. But I'm not breaking out the champagne just yet.'

'Stranger things have happened, but I agree it's unlikely to be the freezer man.' The old man sighed. 'Conflicting facts here. Sign of impulse, but also planning. The open bathroom window and the missing front door key. And a house brick brought to the scene. You've got a puzzle. But coppers like puzzles. How many Rubik's cubes have you had since you were a kid?'

'I used to take those apart to cheat.'

'So take this apart. Knock on doors, find out the victims' recent movements. Search their house thoroughly and talk to friends and family. Get fingers rooting through bins in a mile radius or so, and sheds and outhouses. Your perp might have been watching the place and learned of the key when the delivery man used it. You need to haul all the local CCTV and make sure you pay attention to whoever was on the street when the freezer came. Also, killers sometimes watch the crime scene to see how much fuss and outrage their handiwork produces. So it might be helpful to find out if there were faces in the crowd that didn't belong.'

'Good ideas,' Bennet said in response to these suggestions of routine procedure. Just to please the old man. 'I should have taken a photo of the crowd,' he added with a little grin. Now he turned to the case's most intriguing aspect. 'Both victims had sawdust in their eyes. Laid there deliberately.'

'Wow. Another construction connection. Bricks and wood. Either of the couple got a foot in the building trade?'

'Not as far as we know. Nor was there loose wood or sawdust around. Vicky made a few quid from self-published children's stories online. Mark was a bus driver.'

'You might have a signature killer, or a lunatic playing games with the police. Nothing better for a career. Or worse, if you don't catch this man. This is a newsworthy case, and you were the first man they thought of. Well done.'

'Actually, second. The SIO, a chap called Bates, crashed his car on the way to the scene, so it got kicked to my team. However, there's a DI from the other squad who doesn't seem to like it. She's been hanging around.'

'She? Pretty? Young?'

'Can't say I noticed. The prettiness, I mean. I'd say she's about forty-five. I know DCI Bates well and he's told me about his DI. She's obsessed with solving the big ones. A double murder with a deranged killer on the loose: right up her street. I guess she's after getting her name in the papers.'

Their talk turned to other matters, not murder-related, and when the call was over Bennet accessed his phone's voice recorder to make notes. About ten minutes later, as he was wrapping it up, a knock at his window made him jump.

It was Hooper, glaring in at him with a great beaming smile. Bennet got out. As exhibits officer, it was Hooper's task to attend the post-mortem and collect any evidence found, yet here he was. 'Are you following those bodies? And let's not grin like Cheshire cats at a murder scene, please.'

'Sorry, I got side-tracked by a little CCTV development. And I found something else. I'll head down to the mortuary right after I show you it. This is going to knock your socks off. Follow me.'

9

Now that the bodies had gone, the forensic scientists were swarming all over the house, collecting, dusting, spraying, scraping, and bagging up a whole host of items that needed analysis by a lab. But they'd worked the back door at speed so that DC Hooper could show Bennet the thing that would knock his socks off.

First, Hooper got out his mobile and played for his boss a copy of the emergency call to the police, which had been placed at 0549.

The quality was bad, but not because of the line. The caller seemed to have caused distortion in order to disguise his voice. Over a score of what sounded like paper being crunched, Bennet heard a strange voice say, 'You need to check out 88 Pond Street because they might be in trouble.' Then the caller hung up on the operator.

Hooper said, 'The call was traced to a phone box near Hope City Church at the Megacentre, half a mile north-east of here. So it wasn't a neighbour. Or it was a neighbour who didn't want the call traced to their home. But now look at this.'

Gloved, he opened the back door. Bennet followed him into

a fenced yard the width of the house and twice as long. A thin paved path led to a gate in the high back fence. The rest of the garden was unkept grass, and here, near the wheelie bins, was the old freezer.

Hooper pointed at the window. 'So, you're our anonymous caller. Go have a look at the bodies, as the caller would have done. The two first responders also looked in the window. But they didn't raise the alarm at that point and even went back round the front to knock again. You'll see why.'

Bennet put his face close to the glass but didn't touch it. The bodies, now under protective sheets, lay against the same wall the window was in, two metres to the left. They were hidden by the angle and the countertop. He could see the freezer, and in the growing morning light he could see sections of the blood spatter. But the blood wouldn't have been obvious at the time the anonymous caller made the call, when it had been much darker. From nowhere outside the house were the bodies visible, or any sign that something bad had happened inside.

To know two lay dead inside, a person had to have been inside the locked house. Yet the anonymous caller had known something bad had happened.

10

***

It was her day off, but Liz was wired and unwilling to go home. She considered heading into the station to work on her team's existing investigations, because she needed something productive to do. But she was put off by the thought of being bombarded with questions about what she had seen at Pond Street. It would only heighten her sense of loss. Instead, her mind cycled through other options, until DCI Bates popped in there. Going to see her boss at the hospital was the right move. He would want a friendly face. She would do that.

But en route, an unknown number rang her mobile. She drew in to the side of the road to answer. She hoped it was Betty, the police station café assistant, returning her call, and for once something went her way.

The lady was nervous, as might be anyone sought by a detective. 'What can I do for you? Is this about my son's car?'

A slip there? But luckily for Betty, today Liz didn't care about a little automotive crime, or whatever. 'Well, Betty, I hear you love your bingo. If so, you can help me.'

The nervousness vanished. 'Help you? You mean on a case?'

'I sure do. I have a potential piece of evidence. It looks like a bingo ticket. If you've got a mobile, I can send you a picture of it. I see what might be a number ninety-seven, and a pinkish background–'

'Ninety-seven? Oh, that'll be the Bonanza ticket,' Betty cut in. 'Most bingo only goes to ninety numbers. Yes, the Bonanza. It's a flyer played at eight thirty at night on weekends, and it's got a two-grand jackpot. My friend has won it twice, can you believe? The Bonanza club is the only place that plays a hundred number ticket, as far as I know. It's next to the Redvers House. Has something happened there?'

Liz remembered the Redvers office block. She'd been inside to hunt CCTV because of a nearby murder some ten months ago. The building was barely half a mile away. Her heart started to thump: Bonanza Bingo was close to the crime scene. She might be hunting a local perpetrator, who liked to play bingo. For sure the bingo club would have a customer database.

11

───────

As Liz was ending the call to the café assistant, DCI Bennet answered one from an old CID colleague still based at the Barnsley station where they'd worked together some years ago. After some pleasantries about life, the colleague got down to business.

'Your burned cable restrictor strikes a chord. If it's the individual I'm thinking of, he used an adapted soldering iron. We had a spate of burglaries about three years ago with that MO. Our individual did a stretch of eighteen months and then proclaimed he was going straight. Even got a legit job. Little weasel is back at it, then? Wait a mo, Liam, are you still murder squad? Don't tell me this idiot upped his game and finally killed someone?'

'I can't talk about it, CB. You're going to make me beg for his name, aren't you?'

'Nope. His name's Lewis Carter. And I know where he works and where he lives. You can beg for those, though. Oh, and when you grab him, tell him I said hello.'

12

—————

When the patrol car carrying Liam turned into the rear car park of the Bonanza Bingo club, he cursed. Parked by large bins in a corner was DI Miller's car. The woman was by the bins, squatting, inspecting the ground. He got out and she stood at his approach. She didn't look happy to see him. A second patrol car pulled up alongside the first, but all uniformed officers present remained in their vehicles.

'How did you get here?' he asked.

'I drove. How did you know to come here?'

'I'm asking the questions. And why did you drive here? And what happened to your shoes?'

She looked down at her feet, which were clad in running shoes she kept in the car for driving long distances. 'Don't ask. Let me show you something.' She held up a plastic evidence bag containing what looked like a tuft of paper, no bigger than his little fingernail. She explained where she'd found it and her theory on its presence: dislodged from the tread of a shoe slapped against the wall to shake free blood. The killer must have removed his shoes because they were bloody, which would explain why the footprints ended so abruptly.

Bennet recalled the love-heart shape on the wall and his own theory that a shoe or shoes had been smacked against it. He felt the familiar buzz of a massive clue, but it was tainted with fret. Her actions were a serious breach of the chain of custody. Plus, how much time had she wasted by removing this clue and keeping hold of it? It should have long ago been in the hands of people who could actually do something with it.

'Miller, you removed this evidence from the scene, all alone, and a defence lawyer will tear it apart. Unless you filmed yourself all day, you can't prove you didn't plant this before pretending to find it. You should have called it in and stood well back until it was...'

He stopped. Protocol breach or not, this was still a valuable find, *if* the killer had left this scrap of paper. And she had beaten him to this location. 'How did a bit of paper lead you here?'

'Look closely at this. It's part of a bingo ticket. I thought we'd be looking for a bingo customer. Now look here.'

He squatted with her and she used a pair of tweezers to point. The area before the bins was littered with bits of paper, some loose and tumbling in the wind, but most of it turned to mush and hardened and stuck to the ground. The product of years of dropped rubbish. It was all around them.

'Customers have no business walking so close to the bins,' she said. 'But a staff member dragging rubbish out to the bins could easily pick up a bit of paper in the tread of a shoe. I think we're looking for a staff member.'

'I agree.' He was close to annoyed with her, but it was hard to ignore the fact that she'd scored a point. So, when she repeated her question of how Bennet had known the Bonanza club was a place of interest, he conceded.

'The bathroom window cable restrictor at Pond Street was burned through. A colleague supplied the name of a burglar with that MO. Lewis Carter. I sent a man to his address, but he moved out a few weeks ago. His old landlady reckons he still works here though.'

13

———

In the reception, they gave each other a knowing look when they spotted a poster by the desk. It advertised something called the National Live Bingo Game, with over £10,000 in prize money guaranteed every night. Stuck to the poster was a coloured piece of card shaped like a speech bubble, and inside it said, WON HERE NOVEMBER 26TH. Just a couple of weeks ago.

This early, just after eleven, the reception was empty bar one other customer, whose query was promptly resolved. They stepped up to the desk. Bennet reached into his pocket for his warrant card, but Liz put her hand on his arm.

'Can we join up?' she asked the receptionist. They were told to fill in a couple of simple cards, and for that they got a voucher for cheaper bingo and one for a free drink. There was no ID check and their membership cards were ready in two minutes. Once through reception, they were in a bar area with steps leading up to the playing floor. People sat and drank, or walked here and there, or played fruit machines. A voice over the speakers was calling numbers. Most of the clientele were old.

'Why did you stop me showing my ID?' Bennet said. 'And why did I let you?'

'Let's just have a look around first. If our suspect is here, I don't want him to get word.'

Not how he'd opt to do things, but he liked it enough to offer no objection. Liz approached the bar and ordered a free Coke. 'And the manager. Could you get him or her, please?'

The bar girl said she'd be happy to and went for the phone.

Bennet's phone rang. He spoke only two words, 'hello' to begin and 'bye' to end. When he hung up, Liz stared at him until he noticed. Even then he didn't speak and she had to prompt him: 'Was that call about something important?'

It couldn't hurt to tell her what one of his team had just relayed. 'Delivery man update. He's just admitted to my officer that he went into the house around midday yesterday, and he used the front door key, which the Lawlers had told his company about. But he replaced the key under the plant pot, he says.'

'So someone else took it, if he's not lying?' His brow was furrowed in thought, she saw. 'But what else?'

'The delivery man claims he unpacked the freezer and took away all the wrapping. But he says he put it in place between the washing machine and dishwasher. And he even plugged it in.'

'So the freezer was moved? Our perp moved it so he could put the victims there?'

Bennet nodded. 'I looked in the kitchen window. From outside, that freezer spot is the only place where the victims would be out of sight. No curtains or blinds on the window.'

'That makes no sense. Upstairs would have been better. Or the living room, since the curtains in there were shut.'

'I know.'

People started to file past them, heading for the main hall, as a voice announced the imminent start of a ticket called the

Opening Stanza. The detectives sat at a round table in the bar area.

The manager, a trim, middle-aged lady in a grey suit, appeared a minute later, with a smile that almost convinced them her annoyed-at-being-put-out eyes were lying. They got to their feet and Liz showed her warrant card. The manager looked Liz up and down, and took a long look at the ID card. Even Liz's trainers didn't get as much attention. But Bennet ignored the manager and approached the stairs. At the top, he ogled the bingo floor.

'DCI Bennet?' Liz said. He didn't look round.

'Good evening to you all,' the caller's voice boomed over the speakers. 'Are we ready for some fun and some winning, and are we feeling lucky?' The players gave a weak *yay*. Bennet continued to watch the floor.

'We need to speak to you about one of your staff,' Liz told the manager.

'Oh. Okay. Right. But let's not talk here. Please, come to my office.'

She called Bennet again, but still he didn't move. Something had his attention out there on the playing floor, and she knew it wasn't bingo. She told the manager to wait one moment and climbed the stairs. By his side, looking out over a hundred or so players, she said, 'What's wrong?'

The manager called to them. Liz raised a finger: wait one more moment. Bennet showed her his phone, which had Lewis Carter's Facebook profile loaded.

'Ms Miller? Mr Bennet? My office, please?'

Now Liz's gaze went out across the floor again. From the face on the phone, to the face behind the caller's console.

14

It was a Sheffield crime, but MIT 3 had the investigation and their home was Churchfield Police Station in Barnsley, too far away. Bennet had called his super, who had arranged for a room at the new fifty-cell custody suite on Shepcote Lane. It had interview rooms with video recording and a one-way mirror.

The suspect, bingo caller Lewis Carter, had accepted his arrest for murder with dignity. He was no stranger to the police and knew it was fruitless to resist. Guilty or innocent, everyone caught in the system had to ride the same conveyor belt. As he was read his rights, as he was escorted outside, and as he was bundled into the back of a patrol car, he didn't utter a word. Both detectives knew Carter would remain silent until a solicitor was by his side.

Bennet rode with Lewis while Liz followed in her own vehicle. Both cars parked side by side in the custody suite's car park. In a cruel twist of fate, it was right after Bennet said, 'Perhaps I should take it from here. You head back to your team,' that her superintendent, Roy Allenberg, rang. And now she couldn't avoid him any longer.

Her boss didn't sound annoyed that she hadn't returned his

call. She realised that despite so much having happened today, very little time had elapsed.

'Liz? You're a hard one to find. Did you get my text?' Without waiting for an answer, he told her the story: DCI Bates was out because of a car smash en route to the scene – tore his knee ligament again – and that the Barnsley mob were taking over. 'Where are you?'

'I'm still with the detectives,' was her careful answer. She didn't want to mention that she'd left the location in hunt of clues. 'I was close to the scene and got there before DCI Bates would have. I was securing the area, which is why I didn't get your text.' She described the crime scene. 'But there's a witness who's comfortable talking to me and I was thinking about going there to have another chat with her.'

She stiffened as she realised her error – going there, she'd said, which was a giveaway that she was elsewhere. But he missed or ignored it. 'No, Liz, it's time to head back. Pass on your notes to the SIO there. It's DCI Bennet, I was told. He's a good man. I know you want to help, but his team will do the job.'

'Well, it's my day off, sir. It's no problem to stay and help.'

'No, Liz. If you get deep into this, you may be needed on it in days to come, and your team is still on call. If you don't want a rest day, work on one of your existing cases. But wrap up your handover and come on home.'

Home? He was talking as if she was on a tour of duty in some far-flung war zone. After she bid him goodbye and hung up, she slapped the side of her car. Of all the timing...

Bennet was staring at her. 'This one looks like being long and drawn out. Long hours, lots of knocking on doors–'

'Oh, please. Don't try to convince me this is for the best. I'm off the case by order, so you got your way and you don't have to sweet talk me.'

He took her venom without so much as a blink. 'I didn't say

anything to your super, if that's what you're suggesting. It was your investigation and now it's mine. I'm afraid you'll have to deal with that.'

Her response was to pull out her car keys. Fifteen seconds later her vehicle was racing out of the car park. The reaction was childish, she knew. But she didn't care.

15

———

'Interview room two at Shepcote Lane Custody Suite. First interview with Lewis Carter. Carter has agreed to be interviewed on this occasion without a solicitor. Also present are Detective Chief Inspector Liam Bennet, and Detective Sergeant Sienna Todd. The time is 11.43am on Tuesday the 10th of December 2019.'

Despite a delay to the duty solicitor's arrival, Carter had decided to decline pushing back the interview. Chats *sans* solicitors were great news for the police, but Bennet had no doubt that this interview wouldn't shed much light. Carter would use the discussion to learn what evidence the police had on him and intended to listen lots and speak little. It didn't matter because his body language would deliver a sermon.

From a folder of many, Todd lifted a sheet of paper. 'Lewis, would you mind sitting like an adult?'

He was sat with his chair reversed, arms folded atop the backrest, looking bored. 'Can't. Bad back.'

She left it. 'Last night, Monday, December 9th, you were at work at the Bonanza Bingo club until what time?'

The detectives had anticipated a no comment interview, but Carter surprised them. 'Half ten. Then I went home and slept all night. I'm sure you've got that info right there.'

Carter's manager had supplied his recent shifts, which confirmed what he'd just said. Apart from the home to bed part. 'And when you left at half ten, where did you go?'

'Home, to sleep all night. I just said that.'

Todd selected a new sheet of paper. This one had a blurred CCTV screenshot, which she made sure he got only an angled glimpse of. Enough to make him think a camera might have captured him and so he'd better tell the truth. 'Where were you between half ten and roughly 6am this morning?'

'That would be still in bed, asleep.'

She looked from Carter to the sheet and back again. 'We might have reason to think differently.'

'Well, that's what you people do. It must age you fast, always thinking people are lying.'

She slotted the sheet away. It was an irrelevant CCTV shot from an old, resolved case, here only to unnerve the suspect. They had stills from Old Lady May's camera that showed the black figure in the garden of 88 Pond Street, but they were useless except as proof of due diligence. If Carter saw them, he'd know they had nothing. 'We have evidence that suggests you might have been elsewhere at 3.22am.'

'Let's see it.'

Todd placed her hand on the folder – a ploy to give the impression that such evidence was about to make an appearance. 'How about this morning, the 10th at 05.49am? Where were you then?'

'Have a mad guess.'

'Okay. I guess a spot on Bernard Road, across from the Hope City Church and near the entrance to an engineering firm called

Magnomatics. Both of which are just a few hundred metres from the new address you gave your manager a few weeks back. And what's on that spot in Bernard Road? A phone box.'

Finally, a flicker of nerves. They saw his Adam's apple move as he swallowed.

'Did you make a call to the police from that phone box at 0549 this morning?'

'Not me. In bed.'

Todd made a show of looking into the folder. 'Popular place, the Bonanza club? Got a lot of members from the Sheffield area?'

'I guess. Why?'

'Two of them are Vicky Lawler and Mark Lawler. Here.'

He was shown a series of photographs of the dead couple, yanked from shelves and albums around the house. She gave an overview. Vicky and Mark Lawler, thirty-eight and thirty-four respectively. Mark drove a bus and Vicky made around 200 pounds a month from seven children's books published electronically on Amazon. They had no kids. They had lived in Pond Street for eight years. Bennet's team had learned that the street thought they were a nice couple; quiet, kept to themselves but could be social when prompted. No enemies, as far as the squad could so far determine. 'Did you know them?'

A pause as Carter thought about the right answer. Finally deciding it was harmful to deny, he said, 'Yes. A little bit. Just hello terms. They were regular customers at the Bonanza, mostly Friday and Sunday nights.'

'And do you remember a win they had on the National Game on Tuesday, 26th November? 14,800 pounds?'

A chat with the manager of the Bonanza club had confirmed what Bennet and Liz had suspected upon seeing the poster in the club's foyer. Old Lady May had gotten it wrong when she said the Lawlers had won on the National Lottery: it had been the National Live, won at the Bonanza club.

And Lewis Carter remembered it.

'They received the club cash maximum of 2,000 pounds that night. Remember that?'

He did.

'The cheque for the remainder came into the club for collection on Monday the 2nd of December – remember that?'

He did.

'They bought a holiday to the Canary Islands with their winnings, didn't they?'

Carter shrugged. 'So I heard.'

'They paid for it on Tuesday the 3rd, one week after the win. But not in cash. They waited for the cheque. So, one week after taking home 2,000 pounds in cash, they paid for their holiday with a cheque. There's a good chance they hadn't spent all that 2,000 in cash, right? Good chance that a lot of that money was sitting right there in their house, with Mark and Vicky Lawler still away on holiday. Right?'

'Could be. How would I know what they'd spent?'

'But it's likely they still had a bunch of that cash. Sitting there in an empty house. Is that why you broke in early this morning?'

He said, 'No comment.'

'Did you break in thinking they were still in the Canary Islands, but found them right there at home, having returned early?'

'No comment.'

'And when they accosted a burglar in their house late at night, and found that they knew him, that was bad, wasn't it?'

'No comment.'

'They recognised you and threatened to tell the police. You're out after doing a three-year stretch, so this would put you back inside for much longer. Is that why you silenced them?'

'What? No. No comment.'

'Did you take a weapon and silence them forever, Mr Carter?'

'Get lost. I'm saying nothing. Where's my damn solicitor? I'm saying no more until he's here.'

16

The duty solicitor was a man with two names. His mother had chosen Ronald, but the police called him Villain Whisperer. The solicitor thought it reflected his ability to subdue a wild animal by talk alone, but the truth was more demeaning. Most of the advice he gave his clients was by whisper. The solicitor was by Carter's side when they resumed the interview forty-five minutes later.

New information was still coming in and Bennet had hoped for something vital to hit Carter with, without much luck. Still no fingerprints or other biometric data matching Carter's had been found anywhere in the house. The database had flagged up only a single set of fingerprints: Mark Lawler's, for an illegal taxi touting conviction five months ago.

In the hope that he'd been clocked staking out the residence, Carter's photo was still going around Pond Street and neighbouring roads, but so far without luck. Not all the new information was bad though. Bennet decided to handle the bulk of the questions this time.

Three photos were laid out, face-down. Bennet flipped over the first. CCTV from Bonanza Bingo, showing Carter sitting behind the reception desk. It was timestamped 2021 yesterday. Bennet explained the photo for the tape recording.

'You stayed on reception until 9.30, an hour before you clocked off. That computer has a program called Proverb, which is the customer membership database. You know how to access customer details on this, right?'

Carter no commented again.

Photo number two was flipped over. The same timestamp, but now a close-up of the computer screen. Good enough quality to display the membership details of one Vicky Lawler. Ringed in red pen was her landline phone number.

'This is what you were looking at just after twenty past eight yesterday evening.'

Carter said nothing this time, even when prompted.

Photo three got flipped. Carter captured using the reception phone. Time: 20.55. Bennet showed Carter a sheet of paper and informed the tape: phone records for Bonanza Bingo club yesterday, the 9th of December. Forty-nine incoming, only three outgoing. One of that trio was ringed in red.

Bennet said, 'At 8.55 yesterday evening, a call was made from Bonanza Bingo's reception phone to the landline at 88 Pond Street, Crookes, Sheffield. Owned by customer, Vicky Lawler. You were on reception at that time. You called Vicky Lawler. Why?'

No response.

'Were you calling to make sure Vicky and her husband, Mark, were still away on holiday?'

No response.

'When nobody answered the phone, you decided their house was empty, so, after you finished work, you got prepared and you broke in to steal their National Bingo cash winnings, isn't that right?'

No response.

Bennet said, 'The old back door had a night latch and no key was needed to get out. What I don't understand is why you took the front door key. They kept it in a plant pot outside. Perhaps you knew about it because Vicky had mentioned it at bingo at some point. You took the key, but you didn't need it.'

Bennet showed another photo: the melted ends of the cable restrictor on the bathroom window. But, again, it prompted no response.

'Stop playing around, Lewis. This is your MO, from a conviction for four burglaries. Melted locks using an adapted soldering iron. Look at all this evidence and then get smart. Talk to me. Admit what we already know, Lewis. You broke in to rob Mark and Vicky Lawler because you thought they were away on holiday. But they weren't away. They had come back early. They were home. And when you were confronted, and recognised them from the bingo club, you killed them both to make sure they couldn't tell a soul.'

The solicitor tried to whisper in his client's ear, but Carter jumped to his feet and slapped the table, which made DS Todd gasp in shock. 'It wasn't fucking me.' The solicitor called for a recess, which Bennet granted. But before he shut off the recorder and exited the room with DI Todd, he said, 'We'll get to CCTV photographs from 3.22 in the morning when we reconvene. Sit there and think for ten minutes about the right thing to do, Mr Carter.'

17

———

Liz went to a café near the custody suite and tried to read a book she kept in her car. But her mind was a loose kite, sailing away. Try as she might, she couldn't stop her thoughts floating across the city and into a sombre, pale room where a double murderer might even now be confessing all. A career-defining case, and it had slipped away from her. No, it had been ripped away.

Her teacup sploshed fluid onto the table in her shaking hands. Realising she was getting too worked up about things beyond her control, she sat up straight and tried to focus. But, with nothing proactive to do on her rest day, it was tricky to keep her mind off the Pond Street double-murders. Every minute she sat on her backside was one closer to the breakthrough that could catch a monster, and propel Liam Bennet into the limelight.

So when her phone buzzed, she got off her backside and went outdoors to answer it. Withheld number. She figured it was Dan, her husband, because he often hid his number so she couldn't ignore him.

'Hello, detective. Wendy Holmes here, from Bonanza Bingo. You said to call you.'

Liz's heart raced. Despite a warning from Bennet about such behaviour with witnesses, Liz had covertly given the bingo club manager an order to contact her, and only her, if she came across any new information about Lewis Carter.

'I heard in the news,' the manager said, somewhat breathless with eagerness. She explained: upon hearing on the radio of a major incident in Pond Street, and the name Lawler, she had remembered something that could be important. A few days after Vicky Lawler's win on the National Bingo game, her husband, Mark, had come to see the manager about a 'delicate matter involving Lewis Carter'.

After hanging up, she called Bennet. She cut off half of his hello. 'Have you finished interviewing Carter? I have something good.'

'We're in recess. He's denying. I expect the rest of the interview will consist of just his solicitor reading out a prepared statement with convenient answers to everything I just threw at him. What have you got? And how did you get it? Miller, you really should butt out of this investigation.'

'Let me come down with my information. Let me in on the interview.' She bit back the word *please* and waited for that long-overdue threat to tell her boss.

'Run it by me first, Miller. Now, over the phone. And I'll decide afterwards.'

'Not right now. Later. Can I come?'

There was a long pause, but it was followed by a set of beautiful words: 'Get down here within ten minutes.'

18

———————

Bennet was waiting at reception when Liz ran in, breathing heavily. He'd watched her park and run to the doors eagerly. As she approached, he noticed she'd brushed her hair and applied makeup since their last meeting, to stunning effect. He reassessed his assumption that she was forty-five: ten years younger than that, at least. And pretty, after all.

But that didn't alter his impatience. 'So what's this "something good" you have, Ms Miller?'

'In the interview, if you don't mind.'

That knocked him. 'You want to keep it from me? You want me to learn your bombshell as you give it to the suspect?'

'You'll like it.'

He had doubts. He didn't like it already. What if she had nothing? What if she overstepped a line? But he had a feeling about DI Elizabeth Miller and it was this that swayed him.

19

———

Carter showed obvious distaste when Bennet re-entered, but this time *sans* DS Todd and accompanied by Liz. Clearly he was still upset about how she'd arrested him within two seconds of his entering the bingo club manager's office. Yet when she sat down, just feet from him, she registered his approval at her polished appearance. The way he sat with his chair reversed was one of her husband Dan's habits, and it rankled her, but she gave him a sweet smile.

'Why don't you sit so we can chat properly, Mr Carter?'

He turned his chair and pulled it close to the table.

Bennet resumed the recording and confirmed the time and the players present, but Liz took it from there. Both detectives were aware of a sheet of paper in the solicitor's hands. They knew exactly what it was.

'The waste ground behind the crime scene is now ours,' Liz said. 'Cordoned off. Fifty police officers are combing every inch of it. We're talking to homeowners on the estate on the other side of the area, who might hopefully have seen someone emerge from out there early this morning.'

She showed him a photo on an iPad. A photo of Carter's trainers, which he'd been wearing at work. 'You told your manager you lost your black shoes. We think you threw them away. I believe we might find them in that waste ground, or even the river. But we don't need this.'

The solicitor bent towards his client's ear. Both detectives knew the sheet in his hand bore a prepared statement, which commonly appeared in response to a new evidential revelation by the police. Usually these statements, hastily arranged during a break, would contain information that accepted the new evidence, but with a sweetly innocent explanation for it all.

Now, Liz's revelation that Lewis's missing work shoes could wait forced accused and defender into a change of plan. The sheet of paper was slipped back into the solicitor's briefcase. They were willing to delay it in order to learn more about what the police knew, so they could perform a hasty edit.

Liz leaned back in her chair. 'I want to talk about mobile phones. We didn't find any in the Lawler household. We're close to getting what we need about those phones from the service providers. Any idea what happened to them?'

'Why don't you tell me what you think happened to them?' Carter said.

'Well, the Lawlers did have mobiles,' she told him. 'And I believe you took them when you broke in. I think you took them because there might be text messages on them that don't help your defence. Did you call Vicky Lawler on Wednesday the 27th of November, the day after she won money on the National Bingo game?'

Carter said nothing.

'Did you find her mobile number on her customer file at your place of work and text her, asking her out on a date?'

Carter said nothing. He was as stunned as Bennet was impressed.

'Did your repeated texts that day upset her husband?'

No answer.

'Did her husband in fact feel so upset that you were texting his wife that he called your workplace a couple of days later and lodged a complaint with your manager?'

Silence.

'And did he send a text to your phone, warning you to stay away?'

Nothing.

She leaned forward for intensity. 'Is that why you stole their mobile phones after you broke into their house and killed them? Because you knew those text messages would condemn you to appear in a room like this, answering questions like these?'

Carter slid his chair away from her, visibly shaken, and the words seemed to explode out of him. 'You don't know what you're talking about.'

'The search warrant for your bedsit will be with us soon. Will we find those phones in your home? And that elusive front door key?'

'No goddamned comment. To everything you say from now on.'

'Let's move on to the shoes.'

But Bennet's mind didn't move on to the shoes. It couldn't. Something had bugged him about the missing phones, and something about what he'd seen – or hadn't seen – in the victims' bedroom. Now, he felt an internal shudder as if an answer had floated up, passed close by, and slipped away again, like a shark beneath a swimmer. He needed space, solitude, and got up and slipped out of the room without a word, not to his colleague nor to the tape recorder. Liz announced his departure and paused the interview.

In the corridor, he shut the door and tried to soak up the silence, to think, but his mobile rang. Hooper. Thoughts of

missing phones sank into the depths as he listened to his breathless DC.

20

—————

When Bennet came back, he jerked his head for Liz to follow. She left Carter and his solicitor with suspicious faces, and joined him in the corridor.

'My DC just came from the post-mortem. PMI is between eight thirty and ten yesterday evening,' Bennet told her, meaning the Post-Mortem Interval.

'You're joking. The pathologist originally said about one in the morning, you told me.'

'An at-scene guess based on body temperature, thrown off by the kitchen thermostat. But I pushed him for a PMI. So, Vicky and Mark Lawler were killed right around the time that Lewis Carter was checking out their details in front of a CCTV camera. If ever I get arrested for murder, that's the kind of concrete alibi I want.'

'Damn.' She kicked the wall. 'Hoodoo.'

It was a term he'd heard Sheffield detectives use before. Something to do with an old fictional character called Jinks Hoodoo, described as a curse to everybody. 'Like Sod's Law. You're saying Carter was a fluke coincidence, a piece of bad luck, a false lead. Wrong attitude, DI Miller. If not for him, we wouldn't even know about the bodies yet. Carter was good for us.'

'He was there, Bennet, the evidence–'

'He was there, I agree. And it might have been him on the backyard video leaving the scene. But he didn't kill anyone. Carter is a plain and simple burglar. Our killer wasn't there to rob.'

She glared at him.

'The pathologist found puncture wounds,' he said. 'In the necks of both victims. And the Lawlers were not drug-users. We're waiting for toxicology tests. Blood spray at the scene rules out that the victims were already dead, so it appears these injections were to incapacitate, not kill. But it all suggests he came there to kill them. They were targeted.'

She rubbed her head as if it hurt. 'But... Carter... he was there...'

'Yes. I think he broke in and found the Lawlers. But they were already dead inside.'

———

21

Carter and his defender were still seated, waiting. Bennet and Liz sat. But nobody turned on the tape recorder.

'You'll be happy to hear that we know you didn't kill anyone,' Bennet said.

Carter didn't look overjoyed by the revelation that he wouldn't be facing a life sentence, only deeply suspicious. His solicitor said, 'Continue the recording, please. No questions until then.'

But the recorder was left alone. 'So now it's time to help us. No charges will be brought, Lewis. Not even for burglary. And we know burglary happened. We know you were there. I don't care about that. Tell me everything. Just tell the truth, and I promise you'll walk out of here today. Next time you get done for robbing a house, I'll stand in court and sing your praises. So tell me. You found the bodies, didn't you?'

Carter's solicitor leaned in to whisper to him, but Carter put a hand between their faces to prevent it. 'You can go. I don't need you now. I don't want you to hear this.'

The solicitor started to object out loud, but Carter told him to stop and then stood up. 'You got a yard here? And a smoke?'

'Follow me.'

A couple of minutes later, Carter was in the small exercise yard, leaning against the wall and puffing on a cigarette Bennet had acquired from someone in the station. Liz was behind the door, fuming because the thieving little sod had demanded she stayed away. Bennet let him burn half the smoke before pressing him.

'Carter, I need–'

'Yeah, I found the bodies. In the kitchen. They'd been stuffed in that space where the freezer was to go.'

'You went there that night to rob the house?'

'Yeah, I knew about Vicky's National win. She often came alone to play bingo, so I felt she might be having problems with her bloke. I checked on the membership database and her mobile number was there. So I started texting her. Then her husband complained, so she'd obviously told him.'

Carter's cigarette went out, so Bennet lit it again and waited.

'But the robbery wasn't revenge or anything like that,' Carter continued. 'I didn't care that she'd blown me off. Plenty more fish in the sea. But I knew they were going away and leaving the house empty, and I thought it might be easy to take some of their stuff. Some of that National win cash, if it was still around.'

Carter paused here, as if to get his story straight. Bennet prompted him: 'So you called their home number from work, just to make sure they hadn't come back from abroad early, and when there was no answer...'

'Yeah, I reckoned I was good to go. After work, I went home and got changed. But not my shoes, as your mob well know. I got my penlight and I had some disposable vinyl gloves I nicked from the diner at work. Midnight or so, I rode my pushbike down to their estate. I chained the bike to a lamp post and walked the last five minutes. Their street was dead and dark, so I didn't feel the need to sit and stalk the place. I went straight up the garden path, straight up the drainpipe, burned my way in through the bathroom window. Garden gate to bathroom floor, maybe ninety seconds. I stood in the bathroom a bit, just listening, just to make sure they didn't have a house-sitter. But the place was dark and silent.'

'But not because they were on holiday,' Bennet said when Carter again fell mute. The burglar tossed his cigarette butt and Bennet immediately whipped out another for him, eager to make sure this confession lost no momentum. Bennet saw the door open and Liz slip through. Carter didn't seem to notice her.

He dragged hard on his new smoke before continuing. 'My tactic's to look around each room for a bit before deciding which to toss first. So I hadn't touched anything by the time I got to the kitchen. Man, I froze like a rabbit when my torch found them bodies.'

Carter tossed his cigarette in disgust, as if having suddenly lost the taste. 'The weird thing is, people finding murdered bodies late at night might get scared that the killer is still around. I didn't think that. As soon as I saw them two bodies, my first thought was that I would be blamed. Is that strange?'

'I've seen stranger, Lewis. What happened next?'

'I ran, didn't I? In the hallway, I realised I was leaving bloody footprints, so I took my shoes off. I slapped them against the wall to get rid of the blood. They went into one of the plastic shopping bags I had. You know, for carrying stuff I want to take. I went out the way I came in. Right up the stairs and out that bathroom window. But I know the cops put in more effort when someone's been killed, and I didn't want to be seen in the street. So I went around the house. There's waste ground round the back. Saw that on Google Earth. I went over there. I didn't bother with my bike. Must still be chained to that lamp post. I dumped my shoes in a waste bin on a street. You'll want them, won't you?'

'We will,' Bennet said. 'But what happened when you got home?'

'So it was about half twelve or so. I downed lager like it was going out of fashion. I had to blot out what I'd seen. But there was no sleep. A few hours later, I realised I had to call the police, so I went out to a phone box near my house. I knew I couldn't leave it. I mean, there was probably evidence that I was there. Well, there was, look where I am. But I was worried that DNA or whatever from the killer would vanish if I waited too long, and then I'd be in the frame for it. And I didn't like the idea that their families didn't know. They could be laughing and joking as their people lay dead, because I was the only one in the world who knew the truth. Well, me and the killer.'

Bennet stepped closer. 'I need you to be honest here, Lewis. Are you missing something out? Mobile phones. Did you steal their mobile phones?'

'No, nothing.'

Bennet pulled out his own mobile to check something. Sensing her chance, Liz boldly stepped in front of him, into Carter's line of sight. 'You need to be certain here, Carter. You didn't exit through the back door? You didn't walk down the backyard?'

'The back door? Walk past those bodies, all that blood? Are you insane?'

'You didn't take the front door key from under the plant pot? And you're certain of the time? You got home about half past twelve?'

She'd gotten too close and Carter pushed away from the wall to create space. 'Look, I'm telling you what happened. I didn't take any key, and I didn't use the back door. It was half twelve, okay? You said no charges, right? I didn't steal anything. I'm free to go?'

Bennet didn't seem to hear him. He was making fast flicking

movements on his phone. Cycling through photographs he'd taken inside 88 Pond Street.

Carter was pacing wildly, back and forth. 'Nothing, man. I told you. I swear. I saw those bodies and I got the hell out of there. I didn't do anything.'

'Liam? What is it?'

Bennet's response startled Liz and caused Carter to halt his distressed pacing. Both watched as Bennet darted from the yard without a word.

22

Five hours after the event, the novelty had worn off. The Oakland estate residents had gone back to their lives and most of the journalists had slipped away to write their stories. Apart from the odd white-suited forensics officer popping out to his van with a box of evidence, there was only a fidgeting uniformed scene guard to watch at 88 Pond Street's tent-shrouded front door.

Those in for the long haul had relocated round the back to watch the search team that had invaded the waste ground. Hardly great TV or gossip, but anytime now a policeman might shout and hold aloft a murder weapon for the cameras to capture.

The front door scene guard hadn't had a nervous breakdown and the forensics people hadn't dropped a box of severed heads all over the road, so Bennet's arrival was a breath of fresh air. As he pulled up, DC Ralph Hooper finally answered the voicemail Bennet had left fifteen minutes earlier.

'Sorry, boss. The pathologist doesn't allow phones during the post-mortem, so it was turned off till I came out. He's preparing his report now.'

'Don't worry about it,' Bennet told him. 'Did you check what I asked for?'

'None of what you mentioned is on the list.'

'Send it, please.'

Inside the house, scientists were still collecting and detectives were still looking, but the pace had calmed. With less danger of contaminating the scene, Bennet neglected a plastic bodysuit and instead pulled vinyl shoe covers over his feet and gloves onto his fingers. He aimed straight for the kitchen. Most of the blood on the floor had been cleaned up, but it was far from a showroom kitchen. As he gazed at the stained floor in the spot for the freezer, Hooper's email came in.

It was the exhibits catalogue, a record of all items, biological and physical, so far removed from the crime scene, including the details of the time, place and method of recovery. Bennet checked it for personal items of the Lawlers. He wanted to know if mobile phones had been found. He wanted to know what clothing had been taken. And, most important of all, if any suitcases had been removed.

He went upstairs and opened the bathroom medicine cabinet. No toothbrushes were listed on the file, which had been sought for DNA retrieval to confirm ID. No toothbrushes in the medicine cabinet. No medicines or razors were on the list, and none were in the bathroom.

Bennet stepped out of the bathroom. On the landing, the attic ladder had been lowered and Bennet could hear two of his team up there, searching. He called up: 'Has anyone seen any suitcases in the house?'

A woman's voice came back with, 'Not us. None up here. None in the bedrooms.'

The other detective up there said, 'Do you think our suspect stole the suitcases, sir?'

At first, Bennet had indeed thought that. If Mark and Vicky

Lawler had returned from abroad shortly before their murder, they wouldn't have had time to unload their luggage. The killer hadn't taken the suitcases, according to the backyard CCTV, so Lewis Carter would have entered the property to find a couple of bags of goodies already packed for him.

But Lewis Carter claimed he hadn't fled the house with a couple of heavy suitcases.

Bennet called Hooper back. 'Did you get those prints down at the mortuary?'

Hooper's silence gave his answer.

'Hooper, I told you...'

Bennet stopped as he heard an increase in the noise outside. No longer the hubbub of people waiting around, this was the excitement of change. Bennet bolted for the stairs.

As he rushed outside, he saw the scattered group forming a mass that shifted along the street, and converge on a vehicle that had bypassed the uniforms guarding the end of the street and cut through the crime tape. Doors all around were opening and spilling people out. Faces were appearing at windows. Two dozen voices were creating a roar.

As Bennet bore down on the new vehicle, which was a taxi, two people got out and were besieged like rock stars. Their faces were contorted in bewilderment. And rightly so.

Mark and Vicky Lawler hadn't expected to return from holiday and find their home turned into a crime scene.

PART II

23

———

Liz lived in prosperous Ranmoor in a three-quarter-million pound, double-fronted, three-floor detached house with green belt view. She parked her car in the spacious oval driveway, headed in and set the kettle boiling.

The tall fridge-freezer's touchscreen panel was flashing a warning that the orange juice was out of date. The carton was standing in the middle of the oak kitchen table, by a sheet of A4 paper with a drawn arrow pointing at the offending item. She sniffed the juice, decided it was fine and tossed the paper in the bin. As she drank, she used the fridge's touchscreen to reorder orange juice with a single button.

Then, with the internet at her fingers, she hauled up Google and typed MURDER SHEFFIELD.

She'd been following the news since the story broke, reading articles with headlines like CARNAGE IN CROOKES and SLAUGHTER IN SUBURBIA. Some writers accurately predicted that an intruder had busted in the previous night and slain the occupants, although a number of these stories ran wild with motives. Other reporters told a tale of murder-suicide because nobody had been brought out in handcuffs. The two major theories made for confusion, which stoked curiosity and led to the masses on social media developing their own range of assumptions.

There were photos of the house, the police, their vehicles, and pictures of Mark and Vicky alive and smiling. Many professed dismay that murder had come to their neighbourhood. Some asserted that they had seen it coming. A teenaged hoodlum living on Pond Street reckoned the whole thing was a ruse so the police could secretly watch him.

Then Mark and Vicky had turned up alive.

When the news broke, she'd been heading to the crime scene in pursuit of DCI Bennet, and had pulled her car into the side of the road. The delay in identifying the Pond Street victims promised to cause a real headache for the police in the coming days, and it would get worse the longer the killer remained at large. Especially if he killed again. She had sat in her car and breathed a sigh of relief.

In the tick of a clock, the detectives had gone from swooned-over superheroes to vilified fools. Bennet's future would involve answering a lot of questions put to him by his bosses, who themselves would face scrutiny from police review boards, perhaps even government ministers. She was glad she'd lost the case.

Liz lingered on a newspaper photograph snapped of her exiting her car at the crime scene. She was a mess: tired eyes, creased skirt, one suit jacket collar turned up. A far cry from the superhero image she had of herself. A hand confirmed that the jacket collar was still sticking up. She smoothed it down, closed the photo, took her orange juice and went into the living room.

That photograph, which had been online for hours now, should have been a warning sign that this one wasn't for her. It was as if a heavenly force had tried to shift her out of harm's way by crashing her boss's car, then attempted to give her a hint with this photograph. She had ignored both. But, in the end, she'd gotten out in the nick of time.

A shame, since the case could still become something special. But there would be other high-profile murders.

She'd barely sat when she heard the crunch of wheels outside. She stood and glared through the window as a gleaming silver Mercedes GLC SUV parked. The rear doors flew open and twin ten-year-old girls in matching football kits leaped out, buzzing with excitement. When both parents got out, Liz took her orange juice and headed for the stairs. She tried to get her mind onto her current cases.

Perhaps one of those would turn into the one that made her.

24

'I hope you're not driving while talking on the phone,' said the old man still fishing in Kent.

'Hands-free,' Bennet said, with his mobile clamped between cheek and shoulder. 'Did you see this thing on the news yet?'

'I did. The two who turned up dead just turned up alive.'

Bennet groaned. 'In part I blame the pathologist, and I told my boss that. He was a new fellow and he didn't want any prior information on the victims. I've known pathologists to ask for an entire biography, but not this man. He felt it would cloud his analysis. From first sighting he knew the victims were in their sixties, but what he didn't know was that Mark and Vicky Lawler, the homeowners, were in their thirties. I was about to tell him their names and ages, but he cut me off. If I'd just talked for two more seconds, this silly error could have been avoided.'

'That certainly is a mess. The news said that Mark Lawler had been convicted of a taxi touting offence, so his prints are on file. Standard practice to confirm ID, even if you think you know who a victim is. You would have known your dead male wasn't Mark Lawler. You brought your own fingerprint scanner.'

'I tried to. I usually do the job myself, but I got a DC to do it.

But he went off chasing a fresh CCTV lead and didn't get a chance before the bodies went to the morgue. And then he turned up at the post-mortem late and missed the pathologist's initial basic description of the bodies – you know, male, female, *age*. And added to that, when my DC learned the bombshell about time of death, he again forgot to get those fingerprints. In his defence, this was a married couple's house, and we had a dead couple inside. We all made the error of assuming it was the Lawlers.'

'So what's going to happen to this DC? Back to uniform, if it was my choice.'

'That would be unfair. He made mistakes, but they were because he was interrupted by new leads. I've told my super that I'm willing to take a portion of the blame. It's rare to get a suspect in a case like this so early, and when we did I put all my focus on him. I had tunnel vision and it was a bad mistake.'

'The blame isn't yours. Your job wasn't confirming ID.'

'I know, I know. But the whole thing became an awful Marx Brothers comedy of errors, without the comedy, and I don't want any of my team to face official reprimand for trying to do the right thing. I've shown my DC I'm not happy with him by sending him down the drain.'

Down the drain was a term Bennet's team used to refer to delving into the past. Hooper had been tasked with seeking similarities between this latest crime and older ones. It involved accessing various law enforcement software, like the National Injuries Database and the Home Office Large Major Enquiry System. It was all keyboard and telephone work and considered a punishment.

The old man changed the subject. 'How are the families taking it now that their dead ones aren't dead?'

'Happy, you'd think. But annoyed that we gave them a terrible couple of hours. And additionally upset that social media reported it before we could. Mark and Vicky turning up in a taxi was all over the internet in a flash.'

'And now some other poor families are due a death knock. Why did none of the families or their friends or any of the neighbours know the Lawlers were still on holiday?'

'Something a colleague of mine would call a hoodoo. The Lawlers' flight should have been at four o'clock yesterday afternoon, which would have put them back in their house about eight or nine o'clock, as expected. But the flight was delayed until the morning. They slept in the airport, but they'd turned their phones off in preparation for the flight earlier that day and only booted them back up once they'd stepped out of Doncaster Airport. And that was when they got bombarded by messages from all and sundry: where are you, what's happened, are you okay, there's cops at your house, dead bodies brought out. They checked the news on their phones, but didn't call or text anyone, and raced home.'

The old man said something to someone nearby then came back. 'I think you got lucky here. Not getting proper ID was an embarrassing mistake, but from what I'm reading on the news, the public is fast getting over it. Now that they have had their little shock at the mistaken identity, they're fuelled by the new twist that nobody has a name for the victims yet.'

'It will help being able to investigate without that silly error hanging over us. But it won't go away. It'll be back.'

'There will be an inquiry for sure, and if you don't catch this fellow soon, those wasted few hours will be seen as the sole reason why. You better pray the killer doesn't murder someone else today.'

'Gee, thanks.'

'So what were the victims doing in the house?'

'We don't know that yet. The Lawlers have no idea. No one was supposed to go round except the freezer delivery guy. They don't know the male victim and any females they know well of that age group are accounted for. To avoid the media, we've got the Lawlers in a hotel room in Doncaster. Penthouse suite, but they're obviously not happy that they can't go home for a while yet. I'm just heading back to the station now after settling them in and getting their story. And telling ours.'

'Just a second. You said they don't know the male. That sounds like you have a name for him.'

'Correct.' Bennet laid it out. Carl Allen Roddis, sixty-two, from Stannington, Sheffield. He served eight months in Leeds Prison in 2000 for assault on his wife's brother, so his finger-prints were on file. Carl Roddis was reported missing three years ago by his wife. He hadn't been seen since. They'd found an address for the wife and she had agreed to talk to the police. 'I've sent a lady DI to go interview her.'

'Nothing on the female then?'

'No prints on file. We've got DNA but need something to match it to. She's blonde, about sixty-five and five-ten and has a strange tattoo on her lower back, just a straight line about three inches long. We'll be giving out those details later tonight at a public appeal. My super wants me to host it but I–'

He stopped as his phone beeped to announce another call. He told the old man he'd call him later then switched lines.

'We have to be seen to be making headway,' the caller said without even a hello. It was his boss, Superintendent David Hunter, or Superhunter behind his back. 'I want to tell what we know, and we have to do this as soon as possible.'

Following the return of Mark and Vicky Lawler alive, not stabbed and bludgeoned, South Yorkshire Police realised they had some catching up to do, and a disquieted public to appease. A public appeal had been authorised for later that evening, to seek help in identifying the female victim. And to beg forgive-ness for mistakes made. But the super seemed to be indicating he wanted to bring the public appeal forward. 'You mean sooner?'

'I mean I've already instructed Jane to let the media know. We'll do the public appeal downstairs here. Come on back now and we'll prepare.'

He heard a female voice saying something he didn't catch on the boss's end and knew that Jane Turnbull, the media officer, was in the room with him.

'And I want to tell the reporters what we have. Not everything, but most. Because of that ludicrous error with identification of the victims, we have to show that we've made some forward steps. We'll tell them what we know, but perhaps hold back only that the victims had sawdust poured into their eye sockets.'

Bennet wasn't one for challenging his boss, who had solved all forty-seven of the murders he'd investigated before he was promoted to a deskbound liaison role. But he felt this tactic had been suggested by the media officer. 'Is that wise? If the killer sees it...'

The risk was to the preservation of evidence. Detectives loved to nick killers who might just have the murder weapon, clothing they wore during the crime and other evidence kept all nice and safe at their homes. A killer aware that the police knew about such evidence might hastily transfer it from cupboard to deep lake.

Bennet heard the media officer give more advice, although he caught only the word *duty*. 'I know, I know,' the super said. 'But we have a duty of care. There's a madman out there and it only takes one particular pair of ears to hear that public appeal.'

That part was true also. Killers couldn't be allowed to walk the streets just so that evidence could be preserved, so the more the public knew about him the better. The best person to hand you something when you had nothing was a conscientious member of the public. The first murderer Bennet had arrested had been given up by his sister.

'Plus,' the super said, 'we need an ID on that female victim. The priority is to get her details out there fast, especially that peculiar tattoo. Put that DC of yours, the lazy one, on fielding calls. With luck, we'll get a husband call in that his wife's missing, and a wife call in that her husband came home late last night with blood and sawdust all over his clothing.'

25

___

Liz took two sets of stairs to the top floor, and then a ladder into the attic room. Here, there was only a foldaway single bed, a set of drawers with an original Xbox and a TV on top, and a wheeled clothing rail under the roof window. The floor was bare cork boards, the walls papered to look like interstellar space. She sat on the cheap aluminium bed and listened as the family entered, the twins yabbering about their football practice and the adults talking about annoying local roadworks. And then she heard footsteps coming up the stairs. Slowly.

'Lizzie.'

Liz considered ignoring her sister. Gill was five years younger, but overweight and unable to climb the attic steps. But it would be obvious ignorance, because Liz's car was outside and the attic light was on. She went to the trap and peered down. Gill was standing below with Liz's carton of orange juice.

'My daughters – your nieces – just saw the fridge. What on earth was that you left on the screen, Lizzie? A story about murders? I don't need my daughters seeing such a thing. Your nieces don't need to see such a thing.'

'I'm sorry. I was checking something. I didn't think. The same for that orange juice.'

'Yes. Out of date. We throw away out-of-date items first thing in the morning, don't we?'

'We do. I'm sorry. Look, I'll phone up about some flats today. I'll be gone by the end of the week.'

'Home?'

A ripple of hope crossed Gill's face. Liz knew she'd invite more wrath with the truth, but she wasn't about to lie. 'I'm not going back to him, Gill. It's over. I've told you we've grown apart.'

'But you still wear the Blue Nile.'

Liz twisted the wedding ring off her finger. Gill made a real effort to make sure her heavy sigh didn't go unnoticed. 'Such a shame. At your age it won't be easy to find another relationship.'

'That's not a reason to stay.'

'And you know what you get like when you don't have a man.'

How could she say such a thing? Liz had been married to Dan for fifteen years. But she didn't want to voice that opinion. Instead, she repeated her earlier line: 'That's not a reason to stay.'

Liz then gave her own intentionally heavy sigh. 'If you want me to leave right now, just say the words.'

'Whatever. Look, I'm not trying to push you out, Lizzie. It's just... make careful steps in my house.'

'I will. I'm sorry.'

'Lasagne for lunch, if you want some. Half an hour.'

'Thank you.'

Gill turned to go, then thought better of it. 'Think things through, Lizzie, that's all I ask. Treat it like one of your police investigations. And make sure you come eat. You're getting thin. But the makeup is nice. You should wear it more often.'

And with that her sister left. The offer of lunch had sounded a little like guilt. But she'd gotten one last strike in before departing. And she'd left the orange juice carton on a ladder step for Liz to throw away.

Liz lay on the bed and tried to relax, but the sounds from downstairs made her feel unwanted and full of self-pity. She grabbed a new pair of shoes and slipped down the ladder, meaning to sneak out of the house. As she crept down the stairs, she couldn't avoid imagining the Pond Street killer slipping out of the death house. Christ, she had to get that case out of her system.

Gill's kitchen radio was on, loud, and as Liz was about to open the front door, she heard the word *Crookes* from the radio and stopped. Sure enough, the news report was about the Pond Street murders.

Then it wasn't. Someone switched stations. Liz rushed into the kitchen. 'Turn that back. Back to the news.'

The entire family was here, Gill and her husband and their young daughters. All gawped at her agog. Gill said, 'Lizzie, don't shout at–'

'Turn it back.'

Gill, shaking her head, pressed a button and the news report returned. Sure enough, the mention of Crookes was in relation to that morning's murder. Liz leaned closer.

'All of you be quiet a minute.'

She saw Gill's jaw drop, and the kids jokingly clamp hands over their mouths, and Gill's husband flick a glance between both women, as if fearing an argument. But nobody said anything.

The first thing that astounded Liz was that Bennet's team had already hosted a public appeal, snippets of which the news report played. She heard him outline the case and divulge various pieces of evidence. He asked for help in identifying the female Pond Street victim. He apologised for a stupid error that had allowed the police to wrongly identify Mark and Vicky Lawler as murder victims. He also stressed that the homeowners had nothing whatsoever to do with the crime, although Liz knew it was too early to rule that out.

Next to astonish her was the reaction of the reporters at the meeting. Nobody seemed to dwell on the 'stupid error'. They wanted to know if the killer would strike again, and they wanted to know why two people not known to the homeowners had been in that house, and they wanted a motive.

Liz understood why: procedural errors didn't change the fact that a killer was out there. It was the faceless human monsters amongst them who captivated the public and generated headlines, not the luckless who became prey.

Bennet answered the questions he felt able to, deflected those whose answers gave too much police intel away, and generally performed professionally against an excited crowd. At the end, he was thanked for his time. Liz felt her gut turn over. She had expected the investigating officers to be flayed alive, but that didn't appear to be the case. They had emerged from the fire unmarked. At least for now.

Worst of all, Bennet was now the new face of the investigation. He'd be the one who got this case on his record. He'd do the necessary interviews to feed the media machine. He'd get a talking head spot in some crime documentary in later years. Perhaps he'd write a book when he retired. She kind of liked the guy, but right now she was annoyed with him.

'Is this Pond Street thing one of your cases?' Gill's husband said.

'Not anymore.'

26

After the public appeal for help identifying the unknown female Pond Street victim, the stream of calls into the Churchfield station incident room had become a raging torrent. Added to the cranks admitting the crime, idiots trying to get enemies in trouble, and do-gooders reporting suspicious characters, were reports of missing women from all over the country.

But 'missing' wasn't the correct word. One was a woman who liked to walk her dog at ten sharp every night, but hadn't done so for two days according to a neighbour on another street. An arcade manager fretted over a fruit machine addict who hadn't made a visit to the branch that morning. One nameless man called to say his favourite prostitute hadn't been on her corner last night. Many other callers reported women who'd moved house, and women who'd broken up with them and wouldn't answer the phone, and women who'd been officially missing for years.

Despite having a full workload as exhibits officer and having been sent down the drain by Bennet, Hooper was also carrying out an unstated punishment by fielding some of these calls. By order of the superintendent, according to Bennet, although Hooper figured the DCI was passing the buck on that one.

Most of the information coming from the public would be useless, but every single piece had to be investigated. Photographs, maps and actions had to be pinned up for all to see, all of the time. The investigation was a baby so far but already information was tumbling in at a rate that left no one doubting this was going to be a famous one.

Most of the team were on the streets or the phones or the computers, but others had been given simpler tasks. A DC was unpinning photographs from a whiteboard and replacing them closer together because space was becoming thin, while another squashed folders from one storage box into another because they'd run out of empties. A Scalextric on a corner table, for periods of contemplation, had been removed so they could dump files there. There was talk of securing a van to turn into a mobile command unit and park on Pond Street.

Bennet was with two of his team in another room, viewing CCTV collected from Oakland estate and the local surrounding area. Eighteen cameras so far, which together covered almost the whole estate. There had been many reports of suspicious characters around the area on the day before the night of the murder, but there had been little activity around 88 Pond Street.

The only camera close enough and at the correct angle to catch anything distinctive out front of the crime scene recorded only at the touch of a button, and the neighbours only used it when they were out. Luckily, the neighbours had gone out just after 9am and spent most of the day at Alton Towers, so the freezer delivery had been immortalised.

Eleven forty-four am: the detectives watched a white van enter the estate and park outside the front of number 88; the driver then smoked a cigarette in his van before approaching the house. Because the camera was on a house forty metres down the road, the driver vanished from sight when he stepped into the porch to obtain the hidden key.

Back at the truck, he lowered the tailgate and removed the brand-new freezer, still wrapped in cellophane, and dragged it to the door on a two-wheeled dolly. There was no driver's mate. He struggled to get the freezer over the step, but managed it. He entered the house at a minute to midday.

He was inside the house for eighteen minutes. There was a moment when the detectives sat up straight because the driver didn't replace the key under the plant pot. But then, while smoking a cigarette outside the garden gate, he seemed to remember he still had it. Back went the key and up went a groan from the viewing room. Various cameras watched his van drive casually out of the estate.

The freezer delivery got serious attention, but focus actually intensified once it was over. The bodies couldn't have been in place before the freezer, so the killer had appeared at some point between about midday and ten o'clock in the evening – the pathologist's estimated time of death. In that time frame, pedestrians and cars came and went. Descriptions were gathered where registration numbers couldn't be.

It all amounted to a little bit more knowledge, but the recording ended at 2026, thirteen minutes after the return of the camera's owners. If the killer wasn't the black figure seen round the back on Old Lady May's camera, and he'd left the house via the front after half past eight, then he'd been extremely lucky.

One other camera showed 88 Pond Street, and since it was a commercial system above a newsagent's it recorded without a break in ninety-day segments. This made the detectives happy until they watched it. To cut down on data storage space, the quality was low. Great for seeing vandals right outside the shop, but no good at catching killers 120 metres up the road. The video had gone for enhancement.

Two more were of a better quality, situated closer to the crime scene, but their angles captured only a portion of the garden of number 88 and the street. Anyone coming around the house from the back would be out of shot. The team watched until the point where police cars arrived the morning after the murder.

All told, the detectives had video of almost the entire length of Pond Street and the back garden of the death house for most of the entire day and night of the murder. And it gave them nothing.

The killer had found a route to the house that avoided all but one, and he'd arrived at a time when that device wasn't recording. Had he known the location of the cameras? If so, it raised a question: why had he taken no care during his exit by simply strolling down the back garden? The detectives had widened their hunt for CCTV footage and could only hope that a camera somewhere had a better tale to tell.

An hour later, in the main incident room, Hooper had just hung up on a crank, which meant he had a frustrated tone when he answered the next call.

A deep male voice said, 'I feel silly for saying this, because no doubt you'll know already. You have that HOLMES computer. But you do know your murders are a copycat, right?'

'What makes you say that?' Hooper tried not to sound bored. But he was. He was also a little perturbed, because he hadn't yet gotten round to seeking links between the Pond Street murders and older crimes.

'Same weapons.'

'And what weapons are we talking about?'

'Knife. I bet their throats were cut.'

Hooper sat up a little straighter. But only a little. At the public appeal, DCI Bennet had employed the term *neck injuries* to keep things vague. And since it wasn't a phrase you would use to describe strangulation, the natural assumption would be stabbing or cutting damage.

'I can't speak on that. You said weapons, plural.'

'I bet their heads were bashed in with a house brick.'

Hooper nearly dropped the phone. Bennet had also employed the ambiguous term *head injuries*, but here speculation would fall flat. Anything heavy and hard could be a weapon, and a house brick would be low on anyone's guess list. It could have been a lucky stab in the dark, but Hooper felt his hands start to shake.

'What makes you think you're right about this? And what's your name, by the way?'

'It's a copycat. I remember the first one. I was nineteen. Same place, same way. Check old Sheffield murders.'

'Wait a sec. Don't hang up. I need more information from you. How did–'

'More information? You think I'm trying to wind you up? Check old Sheffield murders. Search for sand in the eyes.'

This time Hooper had a firm grip on the phone, but his bowels nearly got away from him. Bennet hadn't said a damn thing about *eye injuries*, because that was going to be the way they confirmed a confession. This was no lucky guess and he had to calm his racing heart.

'Maybe I will do that search. Would you like to come into the station so we can write down what you know?'

The caller laughed. 'No, I ain't stupid. This is all you get from me. You'll never hear from me again.'

He hung up.

27

———

'Sounds like you're driving again while talking on the phone,' the old fisherman said.

'We got some good information about the male victim, Carl Roddis, from his ex-wife. He was born in Stannington in Sheffield in 1957. In 1982, when he was twenty-five, his workplace started to downsize and he moved to London to be with Jenny, who was just his girlfriend back then. They'd met when she visited family up here. They lived in London until about 1998, and then they both moved back up to Sheffield when her mother got ill. But the ex-wife says she never believed he wanted to return to Sheffield, and it's her opinion that Carl left to go back to London when he vanished three years ago. By then they were far from best friends, and there was that assault on her brother in 2000. He went out to play five-a-side football one night and just never came back. And she never heard from him. She divorced Carl for desertion about two months after he left.

'But here's the thing. Nobody has heard from him. He seems to have genuinely vanished because in those three years he's claimed no benefits, he's been on no electoral roll, and he hasn't worked. But the post-mortem stated that he'd been suffering from long-term malnutrition, so he might have been living rough all that time.'

'Have you spoken to any friends of his back in London?'

'We're working through some names. And friends here in Sheffield. But so far it looks like Roddis's time away from both cities eroded all friendships, because nobody has heard from him in those three years.'

'Has he got any family in London?'

'The wife has plenty, but on Roddis's end there's half a handful. No children or parents. But Carl was not one for keeping in touch with the few scattered ones. Again, the three we've learned of haven't heard from him. However, there's a younger brother who he was close to. Darren Roddis. A few years after Carl left London, Darren left the country. Carl's ex-wife suspects Darren is in America. She says he's physically deformed. Last year they got a Christmas card from him. No address, but a New York postmark. It was to both of them, so that suggests Darren doesn't know they split and doesn't know his brother vanished. It sounds like brotherly love has eroded too.'

'And if Carl Roddis went back to London three years ago, what was there for him if not friends or family? A girlfriend?'

'You're not the first to think that. His ex-wife believed he was cheating on her in the months before he left, although she's not sure he was ever away long enough to have made trips to London. But when we add her suspicions to the fact that Roddis was found dead next to an unidentified woman, maybe we've got a connection.'

The old fisherman clucked his tongue. 'If the dead female is his new girlfriend, and Roddis beat up his wife's brother, that could be a motive.'

'The wife seems genuine and her brother is disabled. We're looking into their friends and acquaintances, but I don't like that scenario. The marriage was over on all but paper years ago and the assault was nearly two decades ago.'

'Okay. And you're looking at convicts in Leeds Prison at the same time Roddis was there? In case he upset someone?'

'Of course. Cross-referenced with inmates who served time there when he did and are now free birds. But it's a long list because unless they went down for serious crimes, most of the prison population back then will have been released. It's been nearly twenty years. And it's not a simple matter to get those records.'

'Well, you've got your work cut out for you. But you've got a good team. Oh, and maybe one extra. That lady who was trying to attach herself to your investigation – DI Miller, was it? Might there be some romance there? It's been a while.'

'You said that already. No, no chance of romance. She's married with what looks like four grand of diamonds on her finger. It's on a professional basis. That said, I hear that she's had romances with colleagues in the past.'

'Work romance is a distraction you don't need right now. You need your head in this one hundred per cent.'

'It is. Look, I'm just arriving home now. I'll call you tomorrow. Save me a fish.'

'I never catch anything. See you later.'

Bennet hung up as he turned his car onto his street, which was two rows of Victorian semis with oblong lawns.

He pulled up in his driveway and exited. He crossed the yard and reached over the hedge to rap on his neighbour's window. An old lady appeared, grinned at him and moved away. She came to the door holding a young kid's hand. He was ten and tall, with floppy hair and his dad's nose, so everyone said.

'Thanks, Patricia.'

Father and son hugged, then went inside. While Bennet found pasta to cook for his son, the boy sat to watch. But something was plainly on the young man's mind. He gave short answers as they ate, until Bennet put their empty plates in the sink and said, 'What's wrong, dude? Remember your dad's a detective before you answer.'

This mild threat usually got at least a wry smile, no matter how dark Joe's mood. Not this time. 'My PE teacher says something called Salvation Army can help tracing people.'

'Joe, we talked about this.'

'Why wouldn't Mum want to see me?'

'And we talked about this.'

He did his best to deflect the boy as they devoured their puddings. Joe was easy to get off the subject, but only because it had happened numerous times in the last couple of years, since he'd begun to miss his mother. At first Bennet had found it hard to talk about why the boy's mother wasn't around, but practice had made him skilled.

Over time, though, he had begun to see Joe's point. The reason she'd left was one he still understood. But it made no sense why she wouldn't want anything to do with her own flesh and blood ten years later. Increasingly, he'd begun to wonder if he should...

But that was for another day. Today, he had something else important on his plate. Speaking of, he got a text from DC Hooper.

Boss, I got something deep down the drain. Thought I'd start by looking online. While I was reading about this old crime, I actually got a call from an anonymous man about the same thing. He didn't even hide his number, so I 141'd it and googled it. It was from a phone in a café in Kinmel Bay, in Wales. Give me the nod and to make it up to you I'll head right down there on my own money. See link.

Bennet clicked the link beneath the text and watched his

phone whisk him across the world of the internet and land at a website called MURDER UNITED K. The dripping-blood font on the title suggested a fan endeavour. A long-time pet project by a true crime fanatic. The link took Bennet to a section entitled: MURDER>UNSOLVED>SHEFFIELD>POSTWAR. Entry #225 in a list of unsolved murders in Sheffield since the end of World War Two. What the hell was this silliness?

Prostitutes get a bum deal, folks. Jack the Ripper, the Suffolk Strangler, the Yorkshire Ripper, all targeted ladies of the night in their thirst for blood. Not all street girls are victims of a serial killer, though, as the murder of Holly Ryan shows. On June 23rd, 1979, the 23-year-old's body was found in the yard of Harrison's Timber Merchant in Sheffield. Her throat had been cut and her head caved in with an undisclosed blunt object, presumably a piece of timber or a brick from the location. And her eyes had been filled with sawdust. Despite a massive manhunt headed by South Yorkshire police, no one was ever convicted or even arrested for the killing. The lead detective was Inspector Iain Jackson. Unfortunately for Holly, missing this date with a murderer would not have given her a long life, because she had womb cancer.

'Okay, Dad?'

Bennet read the article again, just to make sure he hadn't imagined it. But it was real. Here, on a tacky website, was something his own team had somehow missed: a similar murder from years before. Not just similar though.

'Dad? You all right?'

'Yeah, son, sorry. I just...'

Throat cut, head bashed in. Eyes filled with sawdust.

Identical. But forty years earlier.

He called Hooper back. While it rang, he asked Joe if the boy minded spending the night at Patricia's. Joe gave a thumbs up, over the moon about the idea, although Bennet felt a pang of regret. He'd only just gotten back and now he was about to race off again. But it was important.

Hooper didn't pick up. Bennet sent a return text.

Calm down and don't go gallivanting off anywhere just yet. Coming with you. Arrange for the police up there to meet us. Find out if Inspector Iain Jackson is still around. I want to talk to him. See if you can find where the files on the Holly Ryan murder are stored. And get more details on this murder, not just a silly website article.

28

J oe was allowed his Xbox for the remainder of the evening, and Patricia loved to have him over, so the babysitting arrangement was agreed by all within a minute of Bennet's text to DC Hooper. Bennet bid bye to both as they sat in the kitchen at the back of the house, with Joe consuming a second chocolate pudding.

Bennet plucked a packet of sausage rolls from the fridge and went for the front door. As he opened it, he spotted someone storming up his path. Bizarrely, it was DI Liz Miller, and she looked far from happy.

Before his whirling brain could guess why she was here, she thrust a finger towards his face. He took a step back, into the house.

'A distraction, that's what you said I was?' she hissed. 'An annoying fly buzzing around what wasn't my business?'

He had no idea what she was talking about. It sounded as if her boss had warned her against invading the Pond Street investigation, but he hadn't made a complaint. And certainly hadn't used words like–

'Don't we detectives refuse to listen to rumour?' She took a step forward, into his house. He moved back another step. Then another as she closed the distance. 'Don't we ask questions to ascertain facts, instead of jumping on the rumour bandwagon?'

He couldn't think of a response, so said nothing. He stepped back again, and she followed, finger first and mouth a close second.

'Yet in this case you listened to rumours about me and believed them. What kind of detective does that make you?'

'I don't know what you're talking about,' he said, still backpedalling.

'What number did you hear? Thirty? Forty? I've been at four different stations, so that will be a lot of men, won't it? I'm a DI, so I must have slept with my coach during training, and my inspector to get a sergeant's badge. Perhaps you think I'm bedding my super to take his shoes when he retires? For your information, sir, I am married.' She held up her left hand. But he saw no four grand of diamonds on her finger.

Realising, she started to fumble in a pocket, but then froze as she looked past him. With a sinking stomach, he realised why.

They had moved right down the hall and into the kitchen. Joe and Patricia were staring at them. His immediate thought was that no woman bar Patricia had ever been in his house since Lorraine left, no mother-figure, and he feared this scene would mess with Joe's head.

'Outside, DI Miller, now, please.'

She turned and left, and he followed. When she ran around her car and jumped behind the wheel, he leaped into the passenger side. Refusing to face him, she extracted her wedding ring from a pocket and tried to jam it on her finger. Exasperation wavering her hand, she dropped the ring on the first try. He watched the entire process before speaking.

'I heard the rumour you're talking about, DI Miller, and I didn't give it a second thought. I know you're married. And if your boss pulled you away from my case, it's because it's been reassigned and you now have no role. I didn't make a complaint, and certainly not based on your sex life. You need to explain yourself.'

All the exasperation had flushed away, leaving behind meekness. 'Someone told my super to keep me away from you, because I was likely to try to get onto this case by seducing you. That past relationship... I've been a police officer a long time, doing long hours, and sometimes we get close to people we spend all day around. It's just natural.'

'You don't have to explain.'

'This all started by rumour. I've been carrying that floozy label around for years now. It follows me like a bad smell. You heard that rumour and you believed it. You didn't even ask. You didn't collate facts. You assumed.'

'I wasn't aware of any of this, Liz. But what I do or don't believe isn't the issue here. You didn't accuse me of thinking. You accused me of spreading rumours. I haven't said anything. I don't gossip.'

Now she looked at him. 'But one of the probationers at an old station of mine did. A snotty little fool who I'd told off. I reported this new recruit and another man after I saw them sledging down a muddy hill out back of the station, on riot shields. It was Ralph Hooper, one of your DCs.'

'Hooper is for sure a fool,' Bennet said. It was all he could think of. Hooper had told him about an old boss who'd reported him. And that the same boss had slept her way up the ladder. He felt his throat dry up, because he had indeed believed Hooper's talk.

But Hooper didn't know that DI Miller had been active on the case since learning she was off it. Only one other person did.

She rubbed her forehead. 'God, I'm so sorry I burst in like

that. You could have screamed at me. Should have. I guess the unflappable description about you is true.'

'Maybe I'm still numb from it all.'

She apologised again. Thinking of the case gave him an idea how to appease her. He pulled out his phone and showed her the Murder United K website, and the story of the murder of a young prostitute called Holly Ryan in a Sheffield woodyard in June 1979.

Liz didn't question what he showed her, she just read. As the crucial details were absorbed, she exhibited the same amazement he had upon learning the tale. Throat cut. Face bashed in with a blunt object.

Eyes filled with sawdust.

'We got an anonymous tip-off that Pond Street was a copycat. Hooper found this story. We've traced the call to a phone in a café in Wales. I was thinking about heading down there with Hooper.' He paused here. Was this a bad idea? He'd just warned Hooper about not gallivanting off on a whim. His next words might turn out to be a bad idea, but he said them anyway. 'But Hooper's going nowhere. That means I need another passenger.'

He was pleased to see the pretty smile return to her face.

29

———

'You better not be driving again while on the phone, son.'

This time he was parked, but he said, 'I am. A hundred miles an hour, talking to you with one hand and eating with the other. You had no right to call Liz's boss and complain.'

Bennet's father said, 'I knew Allenberg when he was just a sergeant. I didn't convince him of anything, just stated the facts, and he agreed. It's a distraction. You don't need it. Concentrate on your job. Rise high.'

'Like you said, that's why Mum left you. A cliché, but true: you were married to the job, no time for the family. Still are, which is why we have these chats about my cases.'

'I miss the job, yes. But I'm still sharp. How many crimes have I helped you solve?'

His phoned beeped: call waiting from DC Hooper. 'You are sharp, and you are helpful. But you need to keep out of my personal business. Look, I've got to go. I'll call you later.'

What Hooper had to say didn't lighten Bennet's mood: 'The case files from the Holly Ryan investigation were shifted around as police stations closed throughout the years and they're now kept in the National Archives. But that means a trip to Surrey.

But I did find out about the SIO on that case and have some good news there. Inspector Jackson died of a heart attack just a few years after the murder. But his son is now a cyber investigator with the North West Regional Crime Unit, and from what I hear he's got an extensive memory of all his dad's old cases. I've sent him your email address and mobile number. So he might contact you.'

Bennet hung up as Liz exited her flashy house with her handbag and wearing a fresh suit, and again he saw just how attractive and young she was. This drove home a truth he'd refused to admit. This trip to Wales was work, but it was also an excuse to be near Liz. Like a date. Before she reached the car, he slipped a deodorant out of the glovebox and slyly sprayed himself.

30

___

Liz offered to drive, admitting that she was a bad passenger and didn't like to talk in case she distracted the driver. But now that Bennet had decided Liz was nice and attractive, he reverted to a shy schoolkid and it was he who sat in the passenger seat and couldn't think of anything to say. He wanted to ask about her past, her hobbies, her plans for the future, but was wary of broadcasting his interest in her. So, he chose to talk shop.

He plugged his mobile into the dashboard dock and inserted earphones. She looked puzzled until he said, 'Audio copy of the pathologist's report for the unknown female.'

Without warning, she drew the car to a stop at the kerb and got out. He was confused and assumed he'd done something wrong, until she came around and yanked open his door and said, 'You drive. I have to make notes.'

They swapped places and the car moved on. Liz snatched up one of the earpieces. She laid a notepad from her handbag on her lap. They had to lean closer together to both use the earphones, which he liked. But even though it was a condensed, layman's version prepared for the investigating team, the report was still thirty minutes long, and he didn't like the idea of ignoring her for that length of time.

In conclusion, the pathologist asserted that both victims had been beaten about the face and head with a house brick, with nine separate heavy strikes each. Then, before death, their throats had been cut with a knife with a smooth blade. These injuries had occurred while they were lying down, in the freezer space, and one at a time: head, throat, then on to the next. Then the bodies had been raised into sitting positions and slid backwards on their butts to lean against the wall.

There was no evidence of defensive movements during the attack, probably because of massive inebriation – the toxicology tests had come back: isopropyl alcohol, or rubbing alcohol, had been injected into the victims' necks. If they were lucky, they'd been drunk to the point of unconsciousness when they were killed.

The lacerated backs of each left hand were not defensive wounds, but were consistent with a back and forth scraping by a *serrated* blade dragged side to side. So, at least two knives were employed in the murders, although there was no evidence of more than one killer. Bleeding from these wounds suggested they predated the other injuries, suggesting torture. There were various other minor cuts and scrapes and bruises and fractures, but all much older and unconnected to the crime.

After the audio report ended, Bennet looked at Liz's notepad and saw that she'd only scribbled a few lines. And of those, only one had intrigued her sufficiently to warrant underlining.

LEFT HAND INJURIES.

She tapped her words. En route to her house earlier, Bennet had updated Liz on what they knew about the male victim, Carl Roddis, and the theory that the unidentified female could be a secret girlfriend. 'Both left hands. Perhaps the lovers had the same tattoo?'

Bennet had wondered the same thing. The pathologist had speculated that the hand wounds could be evidence of torture, but the DCI wasn't on board with that notion. Someone as barbaric as their killer, and seeking to hurt, would have been far crueller than to mash up the back of someone's hand. And had been. But Liz's idea that the killer had tried to remove a clue to his identity, or show his disdain for the dead couple's love affair, was palatable. He told her it was an angle his team was working on.

He reached over to tap a different line on her notes.

NINE BLUNT FORCE STRIKES.

'The pathologist was quite precise,' Bennet said. 'Not approximately nine. Exactly nine. Each. That seem intentional to you?'

She looked at her written line, thinking. 'Nine Circles of Hell in that Dante book.'

'Nine Rings of Power for the men of Middle-earth in *The Lord of the Rings.*'

'Cloud nine.'

'A stitch in time saves nine.'

'You've thought about this already. You've gone the whole nine yards.'

'Maybe I did some googling while you were getting dressed to the nines.'

She laughed. He put the earphones away, deciding he was now loose enough to raise some of those questions he'd been eager to put to Liz.

31

'I didn't say anything to your super about you. It was my father.'

Liz looked away from the countryside beyond the window as the car sped west along the M67 near Godley Reservoir. She had spent the last few minutes trance-like, except for digging her fingers into her door or seat every time the car ahead braked or Bennet switched lanes. For about ten miles now, he had tried to build the courage to bring up this subject.

'Your father?' she asked.

'He was a DCI in Sheffield. He solved all but one of his forty-nine murder cases. His final one was still unresolved when he had a stroke and had to leave the police. He was only fifty-three.'

'I don't understand the connection.'

'He misses the job. He's always asking about my cases. I chat to him on the phone about them. I pretend I need his advice, just to keep him happy. I mentioned you. He knows a lot of people still in the service. I'm guessing he must know your super from way back.'

'So he complained because...'

Bennet shrugged. 'Maybe he thought, like you were told, I didn't need a distraction. You're not a distraction.'

Bennet pulled into another lane to pass a truck carrying a bulldozer; she watched it fall behind before responding. 'I only slept with one colleague in all my fifteen years, Liam–'

'No, you don't have to explain. You're married now.'

She looked down at the ring on her finger. And then took it off. 'It's just for show. We've split. The relationship has run its course, as they say. He likes his drinking nights out with friends too much for my taste. He's younger than me. But I'm a fine one to talk, with the hours I do, especially on call. I walked out about three weeks ago. I've been living with my obnoxious sister in her mansion and feeling like an unwanted squatter. But I'll buy a flat when we solve this case. He can have the house.' She fiddled with the ring. 'I only wear this to... I don't want men coming on to me when I'm working.'

He thought there was more to it than that. 'I understand.'

'One colleague, Liam. And it was just a foolish one-night stand about seven years ago. He just happened to be my immediate boss when I was a DC down at Lancashire police. I got promoted soon after and my whole station thought it was because of the affair. It wasn't. I didn't leave Lancashire because of the promotion. I left to get away from him and got the promotion afterwards, all by myself. I was drunk and stupid that night and regretted it.'

'I believe you.'

'No offence, but I don't care. I'm fine with people believing whatever they want as long as it doesn't impact my job.'

They sat in silence for half a minute. Liz watched wind turbines on a distant hill. 'But what about you? Tell me about you. I saw that old lady in your house.'

'When you burst in,' he said, and gave a slight smile to show he wasn't still smarting over that event.

'When I burst in, yes. I saw nothing in your house that said it... had had a woman's touch. Are you separated?'

'Yes. Joe's mother, Lorraine, she left when Joe was a baby.'

'Sorry about that. The job?'

'The baby.'

Liz looked horrified. He said, 'She didn't want the baby. She wanted to abort it. I couldn't do that. She decided to... give it a chance, shall we say. But after Joe was born, it got harder for her. She said she couldn't hack it. And then she left me. Left both of us. She said she wished she'd aborted him, and out the door she went. That's as much as anyone knows.'

'I'm sorry. That's horrible. I can't imagine what it's like.'

'It was terrifying. I went to work always worried that she'd scuttle off and abort my son, and give me the news when I came back. I would have lost control... killed her. And this is something nobody but you knows.'

She gave him a long look, and realised it wasn't just bluster. He would have killed Joe's mother. Even the unflappable had limits. 'I won't ask again. I'm sorry I brought it up.'

'Don't be. It's not painful to talk about. I just don't like to dwell on it. It's in the past, so what's the point? I'll clear up a couple of other things you might be wondering about. There's been nobody else since. I date, but I never go past the first date in case things develop. I'm not ready to bring another woman into the house just yet.'

She gave a thoughtful rub of her chin. 'Don't you ever wonder if earlier would have been better?'

'You mean get Joe a new mother when he was a baby still, so he wouldn't know the difference?'

'I'm sorry. I didn't mean that.'

'I do think he misses having a woman around. I mean, he might have developed in new ways if a mother had been around. I don't mean that to sound as if he's developed wrong, because he hasn't. He's brilliant, smart, polite. But he's only had a man's input. Having a mother's influence is something he's never known and thinking about it, well, that's dwelling, isn't it?'

'And you don't dwell. Is he okay with the hours you work?'

'I have Patricia, my neighbour. She's alone and she loves taking care of him. That's the mother angle covered, sort of. Anyway, he's got his Xbox and that will probably replace me soon.'

'Have you heard from her? Do you know where she is?'

'Do you mean, does she ask about Joe? No, she doesn't. I haven't heard from her since she left. She wanted her own life and I was always fine with that. But Joe's getting to that age now where he understands that we have technology like the internet electoral register and Facebook and stuff, things that can make the world a smaller place. But she's not on social media...'

He tailed off, but she knew where he'd been headed. 'You think he might try to find his mother one day?'

'I think that day has already come.'

He watched the road but could feel her staring, reading him. It was awkward. He tugged the steering wheel slightly so the car wobbled. She stiffened up, which he found mildly amusing. Given how she punched his arm after, she'd seen right through his little trick. 'Supposedly you don't do annoyed. But you're annoyed with me right now.'

'I expect a detective to ask questions.'

'I've got an Xbox too. Maybe I should play Joe some time.'

That made him feel a little uneasy and a glance left confirmed the presence of that same emotion on her face. Too close to talk of a date, a relationship, cohabitation... stepmotherhood. They endured another period of silence until Bennet had to slow down at roadworks. Liz grabbed the handle above the door as if the bottom might fall out of the car. His reward for laughing at this: another whack on the arm.

'That's not funny, Liam. Instead of trying to give me a heart attack, why don't you tell me why you joined the police?'

'I wanted to serve the country. I didn't just want a job working for some fat cat's company. But my parents didn't want me in the army. It was that or become a binman.'

'Nothing wrong with being a binman.'

'Couldn't hack all that walking. What about you?'

'My parents both worked as doctors in A and E. Long hours, called in at a moment's notice sometimes. I didn't see them much, rarely together. I was brought up mostly by my sister. It's why she tries to control me even today. I started to hate crime, because often they were gone at weekends because of city centre violence on nightclub nights. I wanted in the police from about age seven. I wanted to nick criminals. I thought of the police as real-life superheroes. Kids my age wanted to be Wonder Woman. I wanted to be Sherlock Holmes. I made a citizen's arrest of an adult shoplifter when I was ten. Beat that.'

'I was three days into my police training when I prevented a murder.'

'Wow, tell me all about it,' she said, and he did.

32

———

'We don't need help,' Liz said, as Bennet turned his vehicle into a car park.

He parked. 'What do you mean?'

'We're just having a look, Liam. We don't have a suspect yet. It's not as if we're here on an arrest warrant.'

'You want to do this without their knowledge?'

'We can investigate and make arrests in Wales. We don't need them.' She nodded at the building ahead of them.

Bennet looked at the police station. He had called ahead to inform North Wales Police of his intention to investigate an establishment on their patch, and had been offered help: escorts, an interview room if they needed to question someone, and a cell in case those questions didn't extract satisfactory answers. He had agreed to meet a pair of detectives right here. They would be waiting for his arrival, perhaps already wearing their coats.

'What about courtesy? It's disrespectful to cut them out.'

'We go have a look, and if we need help we come fetch it. We're just wasting everyone's time if there's nothing going on at the café.'

There was a hint of pleading in her tone, and he wasn't fooled by her claim that this detour wasted time. She wanted to make sure the Welsh coppers didn't snap up some of the glory in this high-profile case. But contrary to what even her own boss, DCI Bates, had said, Bennet knew it wasn't about glory. She just wanted respect; for people to look past the shiny blonde hair and the pretty smile and see the bones of a good detective.

He didn't care about the glory, actually wanted to avoid it. But he had to admit there was something a little thrilling about the idea of chasing this lead alone, miles out of their territory.

As if reading his mind, she said, 'There's only me here, so you don't need to act the strait-laced, cool detective. Come on, if we do this I'll buy you a drink, and I won't tell your team their apparently unflappable boss keeps a swear box hidden in his car.'

So she'd seen that, despite his efforts to hide it when he did a quick tidy of the vehicle before allowing her inside. 'Minor road rage. Doesn't count. And I don't actually swear. And it's not an act, by the way.'

Liz grinned. 'Sure, okay, right.'

Bennet started the car. 'We'll do it your way.'

'Good boy. So where do you want to go for our drink?'

'That's not why. I just don't like the idea of you losing out on getting your face in the papers when this is solved.'

She punched his arm. 'That's not what I'm after.'

'Sure, okay, right.'

The Crossroads Chophouse, end establishment in a shopping parade on the junction of Foryd Road and Bronwen Avenue, just four hundred metres from the sea, was closed at this time. But there was activity.

Bennet parked in the nearby Asda car park. Liz delved into her bag and extracted cotton pads and a bottle of something. Fascinated, he watched as she started to wipe her lipstick off.

'What are you doing?'

'I feel sticky. Don't watch, please.'

He got out of the car to wait. When she joined him, all of her makeup was gone and her hair was in a ponytail, just like the first time they'd met. However, he'd glimpsed her prettied up and it was impossible to unsee. She was still very attractive and still looked young. He also had a suspicion these were attributes she was trying to counter.

They crossed the junction on foot. The café was painted white, with a door right on the corner, where two streets converged, that said CROESO/WELCOME above it. But the door was shut and unwelcoming. They looked in a side window that had a menu in stick-on letters.

There was a single counter lamp illuminating the interior, allowing them to see a man who was stacking chairs upside down on top of tables. He was skinny in the arms and neck, but had a big belly straining against his T-shirt. He looked to be about seventy years old.

'This guy would have been about thirty when the woodyard murder occurred,' Liz said, somewhat dejected.

'I know.' Bennet was on her wavelength: the anonymous caller had asserted that he was nineteen when the murder occurred. She pointed at words under the title on the menu: FAMILY-RUN BUSINESS. He got this, too. The old man inside was the right age to have a son who might have been nineteen when a prostitute was cut down in a woodyard forty years ago.

'Counter phone,' she said. He looked. There seemed to be no payphone, but beside the counter, near the cash register, was a wall phone. He pointed out a CCTV camera watching the shop from above a doorway behind the counter.

'If the caller was a customer, we'll need to see that CCTV footage. If the owner has something or someone to hide, we might need a warrant.'

'We could lie about having a warrant and be watching that video within minutes.'

Ignore the rule book? Before he could warn her against such thoughts, there was a shout from inside the café.

'Closed. Look. Open at eight tomorrow.'

The old man inside was staring at them, shaking his head.

The two detectives looked at each other. On the drive here they had listened to the recorded call, emailed by Hooper to Bennet, and knew they'd recognise the caller's voice if they heard it again.

They just had.

34

The café owner pulled down three chairs at a corner table, flicked on the lights and then went to make coffee for his guests. Bennet had patience, but he could see that Liz was bristling. She wanted to get right to it. She was also half out of her seat as she watched the owner brew coffee behind the counter, as if ready to leap in pursuit if he fled out the back door.

'Calm down,' Bennet said. 'He's too old to start jumping over fences. And he told us he made the call.'

When the owner had answered their knock and they'd held up their warrant cards, he'd deflated, as if he knew the game was up, and told them, 'Ah, so you traced me. Wish we had that sort of tech way back. Yeah, that was me. I called your station. Name's Charles Hardy. You're way off patch coming here, so I guess we'll be having this interview here and not in a station. Sit and I'll whip up coffee.'

Liz tried to relax, but it didn't look genuine. She fidgeted.

A couple of minutes later, Hardy slapped three coffees on the table and squeezed into a chair, facing them. It was cramped, with Liz and Bennet so close their legs touched. But Bennet reckoned Hardy had chosen a wall table so he could keep both detectives right before him, not either side, surrounding him, which they would have preferred.

'Mr Hardy, how did–' Liz started, but Hardy held up a hand to halt her. After he'd sipped and remarked upon the top quality of his coffee – 'best in the cove' – he said, 'Let me just see those IDs again.'

When both held out their warrant cards, Bennet watched Liz's face. Because Hardy only looked at Liz's ID. Nice and long. 'Detective Inspector Miller will be asking the questions. I'll just be taking notes.'

Liz tapped his leg and when he looked, she gave him a grateful thumbs up below the table.

'You're here wondering how I knew them two cases was connected, right?' Hardy said, now focused on Liz.

She ignored that question. 'You said you wished we had had that sort of tech way back. *We*. Were you a police officer?'

When Hardy nodded, Bennet mentally applauded Liz: she'd made a connection he'd missed. 'Yep, I was a cop back when it happened. In Sheffield. I've been here about forty years now, you know. But the wife, she died on me a few back. Before then, no plans to return, hated the place even. Then she left me and I got homesick. Just like that. Overnight. I follow the English news now. I mean, it's all Britain, but this place, this sun and sand, it's like another world.

'Anyway, I saw it on the news. Knew it was a copycat killing. But the news made no mention of a brick murder weapon, you're thinking. You're thinking, how did I know? Right?'

'If you were a police officer, you know the drill. Keep back some details that only the perpetrator would know. Details that you somehow knew. So, since you've been up front with us, I'll ask you right out. Are you the man we're after, sir?'

Often such a direct question fielded abuse, but not always. Bennet had known killers make a big deal of trying to conceal their crimes, only to have a change of heart when the police were at their door. Hardy considered Liz's question long enough to make Bennet wonder if a full admission was about to spill forth.

'Do you want to confess everything?' Liz pressed into the silence as Hardy sipped again. 'You'll tell us eventually. Why not here, where you're comfortable? Drinking the best coffee in the cove instead of the nasty machine-sludge they have in police stations.'

Hardy put down his drink and slowly stirred it. 'What, you think I got something terminal and need to get it all out? Like I'm after a path into heaven? Nah. I'm not your killer. Like I said on the phone, I just wanted to make sure you fellows knew you were dealing with a copycat. I was a copper on the first murder. I responded to it. My first big one. Fresh in the job. I might have info that could help. I was all secrets on the phone because if you came and found me, meant you'd listen and take me seriously.'

'Fresh into the job?' Liz said. 'You said you were nineteen years old, right?' Hardy sipped and nodded. 'But a nineteen-year-old in 1979 would be only fifty-nine today. And, no offence, but you look a long way past fifty. Sir.'

Hardy looked puzzled. '1979? What are you talking about?'

Bennet had a sinking feeling. Was Hardy making his first baby steps into a denial? Or did he have dementia? He stepped in with, 'Just repeat for us, please. You made a phone call about the connection between a current investigation and one involving the murder of a prostitute in Sheffield in 1979. Is that right?'

Hardy's puzzled frown intensified. 'What are you talking

about? Sheffield, aye, but wasn't no prostitute. Was a man, a man with his throat cut and his head smashed in by a brick. And it wasn't no 1979. God, I was old by then. This was in March of 1967.'

35

Bennet once more delved into MURDER UNITED K's MURDER>UNSOLVED> SHEFFIELD> POSTWAR section. Entry #177 in a list of unsolved murders in Sheffield since the end of World War Two.

The murder of docker Harold Davies on the evening of Thursday March 16th, 1967 in Sheffield was one that terrified the community. Davies had gone out with a friend to attempt to sneak into the Passion Club. How he ended up dead ten miles away is still a mystery. He was found in the partially demolished, now long-gone building of the recently closed Wandle School the next morning by workmen starting their shift. His throat had been cut and his head demolished by a brick or piece of wood taken from the construction detritus scattered around. Sand from the building works had been forced into his eyes. No weapon or motive was confirmed. No witnesses were found who saw Davies at any point between the Passion Club and Wandle School. None of Davies' friends or family had been able to shed a light, and none of the bruisers at his local boxing club had looked good for it. Locals were questioned and a man was arrested but later let go without charge, and today the

*case remains a near-forgotten mystery. The case was headed by
Inspector–*

He let the phone slip onto the table with a clatter. Liz picked
it up and read.

The café owner, Hardy, had gone upstairs to prepare something he wanted to show them. Bennet left the table and went to
the counter, where he absent-mindedly fiddled with a tub of
butter portions.

When he heard the soft click of his phone being laid on the
table, he turned. Liz was staring at him. She looked as incredu-
lous as he still felt.

'The method of death is hard to ignore,' she said. 'But let's
not be hasty to connect all three crimes. Smashed heads and cut
throats, that means nothing. I bet we could find fifty such cases
in Sheffield over the years. Even the eyes could be a coincidence.
It was sand, the website said. Not sawdust.'

He didn't respond.

'So what are we thinking, Liam? This certainly isn't one
ancient serial killer, and I'm not sure I buy the idea of copycats.
Liam? Are you okay? Something has upset you and I can't work
out what.'

'Did you read right to the end? Did you see who the lead
detective was?'

She picked up the phone to check. He saw her eyes widen.
'Is this right? The lead detective... Ray Bennet... he's...'

'Yes,' Bennet said. 'The Wandle School murder in 1967 was
my father's case. The only murder he never solved.'

PART III

36

Hardy had returned with a smile and an announcement – 'It's ready for you' – and now, standing in his back bedroom, they understood his glee. And just how much was out of whack in this guy's head.

The former policeman had turned the room into... there was no other term for it: a murder shrine. All four walls were coated in laminated front-page newspaper clippings, every piece bearing the story of a shocking small-town massacre, a wacky unsolved killing, infamous serial slayings.

These laminates were arranged in a neat grid, with the spaces between the rows and columns dotted with sidebars detailing a police appeal, a criminal's arrest, a sensational trial. Everywhere they looked, a victim or a killer stared back. There was barely wallpaper to glimpse.

But there was more. The ceiling bore a larger laminate, right above the bed, where Hardy could gaze at it while lying down. It was a newspaper photo of a uniformed officer standing outside Wandle School to keep onlookers back. It had been blown up so big that detail was lost, but both detectives knew there was only one reason Hardy would have done this.

The policeman keeping people out of a crime scene was Hardy.

And more still. Apart from the bed there was only one other piece of furniture. It was a small table and it existed only to boast a tiny plinth with the room's central attraction. After dragging their gaze from the glut of death surrounding them to look at one other, each detective knew the other had no doubt what that centrepiece was.

37

After Hardy's arrest and handover to North Wales Police, Bennet drove Liz to Rhyl railway station, where they parted ways.

The son of Iain Jackson, SIO in the Holly Ryan murder, had emailed Bennet with a willingness to help. He would meet Bennet at his home, tonight. He lived in Liverpool, just twenty or so miles away, which was handy. But a land journey had to skirt the Wirral peninsula created by the River Dee and River Mersey, so her train would take somewhere around two hours. In his return email, Bennet said he'd be sending Liz in his place.

He had a different former police officer to talk to.

On the train, Liz took a call from her sister, Gill, and needless to say, it wasn't a pleasant experience.

Gill was five years younger, but played big sister. Always had. As a teenager, when their parents worked long hours at the hospital and left the girls alone in the evenings, Gill had looked after Liz. Controlled would have been a better word. Gill told her what to eat, how to style her hair, and what time to be home at night. She had also tried and failed to select Liz's boyfriends and career path.

But Gill had also been a shoulder to cry on and was servant-like at times, which had meant Liz hadn't really seen her sister's behaviour as a form of control. That changed when Liz joined the police. The police force was for men, Gill believed. Gill wanted Liz to become a mother and housewife with a part-time job. She was very 1950s like that. Or perhaps she saw the police force as akin to healthcare, and look what that had done to Mum and Dad.

Even as Liz rose through the police ranks, proved she was good, and dedicated herself to helping others, Gill refused to see the quality of her sister's place in the world. And Liz started to wonder if her sister was a megalomaniac.

Then again, her sister's current antagonism towards her might be because Liz had made a shambles of the only major life decision Gill had subscribed to. Evidenced by her first words now:

'Dan left a voicemail. You didn't get back to the poor man? Leaving him waiting like that. I don't know.'

'Gill, I don't have to talk to him. He cheated on me.'

As expected, this statement struck her sister dumb. For weeks now Liz had skirted around the real reason why she'd walked away from her husband, using terms like *run its course* and *grown apart*. It had invited scorn from her sister, but Liz hadn't wanted to smear the holier-than-thou image Gill had of Dan. Well, no more.

'Don't be silly,' Gill said eventually. 'What is this, detective brilliance? He was texting in the toilet, was he? That's why you assume–'

'He was in a café with another woman. They were holding hands. A police dog could work that one out.'

'Well, you could still be wrong.'

Gill didn't sound so sure now. Liz said, 'Perhaps I am. He is the perfect man in your opinion, after all. I'll talk to you later. I'm on a case.' And with that she hung up.

38

———

Many miles south of Liz, Bennet called his son because it was approaching his bedtime. Patricia, the elderly neighbour, called Joe down from the bathroom to take the call.

They spoke about school, and Xbox, and what plans Bennet had for the garden, and when he found a suitable moment, he said, 'Joe, do you remember that woman who came into the house today? The one it looked like I was arguing with. We weren't arguing, by the way. But what do you think about if I invite her for dinner? The four of us can have dinner. Afterwards, she can play you on your Xbox.'

'Can I stay up? And is she staying? Can she sleep in my room?'

'Nothing definite yet. But we'll see. Anyway, I want to know about your violin practise. How's that going?'

Bennet tried to listen to his son's tale, but it was challenging to shift his mind off what he'd discovered at the Crossroads Chophouse. Although he knew about some of his father's old murder cases, Bennet had never delved that deeply into them, but that didn't stop him feeling that he'd made an error in not seeing the similarities. His father, too: the former detective had heard all the details of the Pond Street murders and should have noted the parallels. Bennet was eager for answers. And he would have them soon.

39

———

At Liverpool Lime Street, Liz emailed Xander Jackson, but the automatic reply told her he'd be out at the gym until 11pm, three hours away. She took a taxi to a 24-hour Hertz in Wallasey to hire a car, about six miles away. By the time the paperwork and return journey were done, it was almost time. She drove back, parked and opened her cosmetics purse.

Xander lived within sight of Anfield football stadium, though he wasn't a football fan. He liked to exercise and had his own cellar gym, where he chose to conduct their conversation. He was late forties and extremely handsome, but his peacocking put her off. As they talked, he jogged topless and in tight shorts on a treadmill, while she sat on a wooden kitchen chair he'd placed right in front of the machine.

She tried to concentrate on his face, not his muscular body, or that damn shoulder tattoo reminiscent of the one her husband, Dan, had. The guy had dedication if he'd been at the gym before doing this. Or this part was for her benefit. She wished she hadn't put makeup on for this meeting.

40

———

By this time, Bennet had already passed through Slough, just west of London, and was on the final thirty-mile southwestern run to Capel, a tiny hamlet lost in fields and just a mile from Tricklebrook Fishery. Here, he pulled over and made a call to a mobile. 'I'm coming to you. It's important you're in.'

Then he hung up. It would give the man he intended to visit about half an hour to get home, if he wasn't already.

Sitting in the dark on a quiet road gave Bennet time to think. He loaded Facebook and typed a name.

He knew that his son, Joe, had searched for his mother on social media without success, and Bennet had allowed him to think she didn't have a profile. But she did. Despite giving that impression to Liz, he'd never married Lorraine, so she hadn't taken his surname.

Now, he scrolled through Lorraine Cross's profile. Since two days ago, when he'd last looked, she had created a post: a picture of her new garden decking almost completed, with a comment that 'the boys might be due a beer in another few hours'. Her husband of seven years was in the background with a friend,

139

both men taking a breather from hammering wood to smile at the camera.

And in her arms was Tessa, her five-year-old daughter.

Bennet sent Joe a message bidding him sweet dreams. Unwilling to yet again let rage the internal debate about the pros and cons of reintroducing Joe to his mother at his age, he slid the phone away, wiped his wet eyes, and drove on.

In Capel, just past a scary-looking graveyard, he stopped at a white wooden house just metres off the dark lane. The lights were on. He felt nervous about this visit to a place he was familiar with. He took a few minutes to compose himself before heading up the path to rap on the door.

'It's about your unsolved,' Bennet said when the door was opened. His father said nothing, just turned and walked away: an invite to enter.

41

‘Twenty-third of June 1979. Harrison's, a woodyard, which closed in 1988, was where my dad found the body of Holly Ryan, aged twenty-three. She was a prostitute. She was found at the end of the entrance driveway, behind a stack of timber. Her head and face were bashed in, most likely by a piece of wood from the yard or one of the house bricks lying around, and while she lay on her back, her throat was cut.

‘There was a narrow, hidden lane from the end of the street and through the allotments to Bole Hill Road, which was where the ladies used to escape if police cars came down the street. The area on the other side of the road to the woodyard was allotments, too, and this was where the ladies took their clients. They didn't often use the woodyard because there was a river that ran along behind the fence and across the gateway. There was no gate, but after closing time the timber workers removed a sheet of metal laid across the river so that vehicles couldn't get in.

‘This was what led my father's team to believe Holly hadn't been picked up by a driver. The driveway was used by people crossing onto Henney Road, a thoroughfare, by going over an embankment and a bridge across a railway. Especially in the evening, when the Henney Road chip shops and pubs and clubs were open.

'There were various suspects, including seven from the woodyard. Three of those seven, because of a history of violence, were put under surveillance. But in the end none of them looked good. Semen traces in Holly's vagina proved she'd had sex within about twenty-four hours of the murder and from this a B blood group secretor was determined. Later, this information was published in police reports, distributed to various forces across the north, asking for any B group secretors arrested to be passed on to the Holly Ryan murder team.

'It was a promising lead right up until a police officer from Leeds read the circular and admitted it was him. He'd travelled from Leeds to Sheffield to acquire the services of a prostitute. He had an alibi. No other clients of Holly's were traced. There were no regulars.

'Only one suspect ever got a really thorough examination. A man called Sam Thomas, a minor celebrity because he was a speedway star who rode for the Sheffield Falcons. According to Thomas, and backed up by some of the local prostitutes, Holly and he were old school friends. He claimed he'd bumped into her at a pub about a year before the murder, and she told him she was on the game. He said sometimes he'd bring her hot meals, or he'd buy her things, and he taught her things like mathematics, because he felt sorry for her lifestyle.

'According to him, he offered Holly the use of his parents' barn on his farmland in Norton. That place was only half a mile west of the woodyard across fields and allotments. He said she turned him down, but used to make the mile-and-a-half trek some nights and sneak in to sleep there anyway. He said Holly believed he didn't know and he kept it that way so that she wouldn't go somewhere less safe. He pledged he never slept with her. But they must have had long, intimate chats because he knew about her uterus cancer before the autopsy revealed it.

'The Thomas family agreed to allow their property to be searched, but nothing incriminating was found, although Thomas's father had a bootleg radio station set-up in the root cellar under the barn. There was no evidence against Thomas at all, except for a weak alibi. He said he'd been on the farm, practising his bike skills, and his mother was the only witness to this.

'There wasn't enough to arrest him though. However, Sam Thomas was back under scrutiny in 1996. When the DNA database was set up in 1995, it was the same year that Holly Ryan's mother died and there was local interest in the case again. Police found some old evidence from the murder and got Holly's DNA from her teddy fur coat, along with Thomas's. He was questioned again, but he said he gave Holly the coat as a present, so his DNA, of course, would be on it. Police did find an old reference to this in the statement of one of the girls who worked with Holly. But there was also another, unknown DNA profile on that coat. But the database was brand new and didn't have many profiles stored. There was no match to the unknown profile.

'Other than that, there were no arrests, no viable suspects. They didn't have a motive because there was no sexual assault and she hadn't been robbed. No witnesses. A walling hammer found near the scene contained no blood or fingerprints and was later decided to be unrelated, just a tool cast off from the woodyard. No murder weapon was ever discovered.

'Holly's red high heels were tossed over a fence onto the railway embankment, but they landed in a ditch of standing water and evidence might have been lost. Her grimy teddy fur coat was found rolled up and stuffed underneath a large water tank about forty metres away. Two grey fibres were lifted from exposed portions of her skin by Sellotape at the scene, and one was stuck inside her cheek, and these were consistent with fibres found on that teddy coat. But they didn't match any of her clothing nor any seized clothing from suspects.

'There was no other good forensic evidence. Five months after the murder, the case was lowered in priority because of separate murders, unconnected, that needed manpower. By then the murder squad had eighty-nine officers working on it, many full-time. They'd logged 48,000 hours. Three hundred and ninety-nine statements had been taken. They'd knocked on 2,000 doors to ask questions. Where Holly was found was an area that delivery vehicles used for unloading and it was a mishmash of tyre tracks, and they'd traced and eliminated some thirty-one vehicles, but many others couldn't be traced.

'The detectives just didn't have anything. It happens sometimes. Today, with our technology, they might have solved that murder on day one. But it got cold and died, fast.'

By the end of his long recap, Xander was sweating and panting. He stopped jogging and turned the machine off. He leaned forward, propping himself on the handles. To make sure his triceps stood out.

Liz looked at her notebook. Anywhere but his glistening skin. 'I'd like to get hold of some of this evidence, if possible. Holly's fur coat and her shoes, for instance. We're having trouble tracing where the items are stored.'

'I know, DNA technology has come on a long way. During my father's investigation, one of those shoes got mislaid. As for the rest of it, I couldn't tell you. They keep shutting labs and police stations. Old boxes get shifted to and fro and things get lost, or not recorded correctly. What's not been destroyed, like the bigger items, might be lurking around somewhere.'

Liz sighed. She'd hoped this man might have some of that evidence as a keepsake. She scanned her notes, seeking questions to ask. Xander stepped off the machine and grabbed a towel. He took the other wooden chair and slid it just a few feet from Liz. He sat with his legs apart just enough to make her feel uncomfortable. 'Your recall is great, by the way. But I'd still like those files, if you don't mind.'

Liz had expected the former SIO's son to have the case files ready for her, but he hadn't fetched a thing – they were still boxed up in the attic. He'd guaranteed that his knowledge of his father's old investigations would satisfy any queries she might have.

'In time I'll get them for you,' he replied. 'But certainly not tonight because they're surrounded by years of junk and it's hard to move up in the attic. Ms Miller, I didn't get traditional bedtime stories. My dad talked to me about his cases. He kept the blood and guts out though. Maybe he thought that was all right. He let me read his typed notes on the cases. All his cases. I got to hear about all his solved murders and all his cold cases. I never worried about alien monsters under the bed because by then I knew the real monsters were my shape and out there even in the daytime. I haven't killed anyone myself and I don't talk to the moon, so it didn't mess with my mind too much.'

He leaned forward, elbows on knees, and looked deep into her, which she found nice and awkward at the same time. She fiddled with her useless wedding ring to make sure he saw it. 'I didn't mean to imply anything. I know your knowledge of this case is second to none. It's just that the case files will have photographs. I hope I'm not opening old wounds here.'

'My dad failed to solve other murders. The woodyard murder was one of many. It didn't affect him, he didn't turn to drink or have sleepless nights because of it, and it doesn't affect me. Those files are locked up in the attic purely to save space, not because seeing them would bring back bad memories. I'll get them to you soon, I promise.'

That would have to do. She looked at the notes she'd taken. There were only two, just like before, after she'd reviewed the post-mortem file on one of the Pond Street victims. The same two.

'Mr Jackson, you say the investigators weren't certain if the weapon was a house brick or a piece of wood. But what about the number of injuries to Holly?'

'One long cut to her throat,' he said, happy to prove his point, 'and between eight and eleven blows to the face and head.'

Her first note said NINE BLUNT FORCE STRIKES. It was possible that Holly Ryan, just like both victims at Pond Street, had received the exact same number of blows. Liz had already scoured the internet for information on the Ryan murder and hadn't found any blog or news item or forum chat that had mentioned a specific number of strikes. 'Was that information put out in the world? The exact number of strikes?'

'No. But not for secrecy. There was no certainty about how many times Holly was hit because the damage was so extensive. So, number of strikes wasn't deemed to be something that could be used to verify a confession.'

She needed the autopsy report on Holly Ryan, just in case Xander Jackson's knowledge had limits. If it transpired that Holly Ryan and the Pond Street victims had been dealt exactly the same number of head shots, and that number wasn't in the public domain, it would weaken the theory of a copycat. Even forty years later, they might be looking at the same offender.

She wondered what Bennet would learn from his father. Would his dad's old unsolved investigation prove to be so similar to Pond Street and Ryan that a link between all three cases was irrefutable? If so, the story would ignite around the world.

'Ms Miller? Any more questions?'

Liz looked at the other note she had written. LEFT HAND INJURIES. She asked.

'Injuries to her hands? Not that I'm aware of. I mean no,

there weren't any. No defensive wounds on her hands or arms. It was a blitz attack that offered her no time to fight back.' He gave a little chuckle. 'You look doubtful of my recollection.'

'No, it's not that. But I really would like those files. The pathologist's report, and all the photos you still have. The only crime-scene photos online are distant shots by reporters.'

He scratched his chin, thinking. 'You don't like this revelation about the hands. I'm guessing the lack of defensive wounds doesn't gel with your current case. You were hoping for a similarity.'

He was on the ball with that claim. There were enough matches between the two crimes to claim a direct link, she knew. But the hand injuries on the Pond Street victims had become a twisted conundrum now that Holly Ryan didn't have similar.

'Look, I'll get you the files and I'll email you,' Xander said, 'but I do promise you that what I don't know isn't worth knowing. You could do worse than use my memory to solve the Ryan murder or any of my father's other unsolved crimes.'

'Mr Jackson, I want you to know I'm not working on a cold case here. This information is to assist with my current investigation, that's all.'

'Yeah, I know that, Ms Miller. There were a handful of times that police officers came to the house about this case, looking for new information. Mum hated it. But that stopped long ago. It's not a case that haunts the public. They don't care. Holly Ryan was just a prostitute and it was forty years ago.' He got up and, unbelievably, started doing squats. 'I'll send you some files by email, but you're the first to come about it in, oh, ten years. I know that nobody has decided a dead prostitute finally needs justice. This is because of that old bomb site.'

'Bomb site?'

He stopped in a squat position. She was tempted to tell him his flirting techniques needed work. 'When I got an email asking me to contact a detective called Liam Bennet, I googled him and found a news item about a murder. Two dead in a house in Oakland estate in Sheffield. The article was entitled UXB Not Biggest Murder Threat, unbelievably. Journalists like to show off their research. The article said that in World War Two, Sheffield was a major target for the Germans because of the Vickers factory, the only place where they made crankshafts for the Rolls-Royce Merlin engines. The Germans were eager to smash the city. Many unexploded bombs still exist there and in 1948 one was found unexploded by twin brothers on what is now the site of the Oakland estate.'

'I don't understand the connection.'

'Then watch your step next time you walk around that crime scene.'

42

Former inspector Ray Bennet led his son into the backyard, where there was decking with chairs, a lamp and a heater under a gazebo. They sat. The view was of nothing but night and wavy silhouette treetops.

'I'm sorry about what I did,' his dad said. 'Calling that lady detective's boss and complaining about her. I knew Superintendent Allenberg back from when he was a fresh recruit and I was nearing retirement.'

Bennet dove right in: 'I found new information about the Wandle School case.'

His father's expression didn't change, but the jaw muscles clenched. A sign of disquiet, Bennet knew. 'You didn't tell me that was being reopened.'

'It isn't. But it might be. Let me explain.'

In 1967, a rookie patrol officer called Charles Hardy got routed to the closed-down Wandle School after a call from a courting couple, who'd sneaked inside the half-deconstructed building to canoodle, about what they thought was a homeless man sleeping. Hardy was a man obsessed with murder, who'd joined the police for the sole reason of getting up close to major crimes. His bedroom was a shrine to all the famous cases. By '79, Hardy had long left the force and long lived in Wales, which was why he never learned about the Holly Ryan woodyard murder.

After his wife died, he started to think about returning to England and began to catch up on English news. When he heard about Pond Street, he saw a connection between that crime and the murder in '67 and immediately called the police. He was delighted to tell his tale and show off his murder shrine. Including that centrepiece...

When the tale was told, his father leaned back, which cast part of his face into shadow. But Bennet could see what he thought was veiled anger. 'This man had the murder weapon from the Wandle case? On a plinth? As a bloody trophy?'

Bennet and Liz had expressed the same amazement upon seeing a broken house brick spotlighted like a rare museum exhibit. There was only one reason why that item would be deemed so important, but Bennet was careful.

'Hardy stole what he thought was the murder weapon, but that doesn't mean he was correct,' he said. 'But I called in the local boys to arrest him and the brick has been seized. It's going for DNA analysis, as soon as we can find something to match it against. I made some phone calls while I was headed here, but I'm having problems locating most of the evidence from your case.'

Ray Bennet took a couple of deep breaths. 'Evidence gets lost even when investigations are red hot, so good luck finding anything from the sixties. That was before things could be typed onto a computer, so you won't find much information in the databases. You'd have to visit police stations and physically open boxes. Believe it or not, I heard about a whole bloodstained sofa being lost once. If we'd known back then that something called DNA was going to revolutionise things twenty years later, there would have been more care taken with stored evidence.'

Bennet senior thought. Bennet junior waited.

'Davies won an amateur boxing trophy at a match at a club, but the name escapes me. I remember they had trophies from matches won as far back as the 1920s. If that place still exists and still has that trophy cabinet, maybe Davies' trophy is sitting there with his DNA all over it.'

Bennet made a mental note of that.

His father said, 'This man, this officer. Hardy. If, like he says, he was the first responder and the one guarding the school's front entrance, then I remember him. As soon as I arrived, he tried to ask me questions and give his opinion. A little idiot, I remember thinking. And this man hid the murder weapon. He cost me that case.'

'It sure didn't help.'

'We put up a massive effort to solve that killing. It was a brutal affair. Harold Davies was found about fifty metres along the main corridor from the entrance, on his back with his face caved in and his throat cut. Right in a lake of blood that went from wall to wall. He was an amateur boxer, but the blunt instrument blows were all to the front, so his killer hadn't attacked him from behind. He'd stood face to face with a victim who was six-three and two hundred and forty pounds of muscle. There were anti-footprints in the blood. By that I mean empty spots. The killer stood there while the blood pooled around his feet. He stood there for so long the blood had partially congealed, which meant it didn't fill those footprint shapes when he moved.

'Davies was a few feet from a set of doors across the hall and they were locked, but his feet were pointed towards the entrance. We got the impression he'd walked down the corridor, stopped and turned. As if called to. Then he'd been struck in the face and had toppled backwards.

'Best suspect we ever got was a man who was lurking near a

garage on a street about half a mile from the scene. He was spotted at about eleven at night, about half an hour after the time we assumed the murder was committed, by a driver of a bus. We interviewed him, but he stuck to his story and we never broke it. He was all we ever got.

'In later days there were accusations against us that we were slack. Davies and his family called him a docker, but in those days down in London people had to stand on the stones, as the saying goes, and hope to get work. But it was infrequent that Davies would make the trip to London and we learned that he loan-sharked as a way of making ends meet. That made him unpopular and on his estate he was considered a thug. There were plenty of people who didn't shed a tear. The police were accused of half-heartedly trying to solve his murder. But that's just not true. We gave it our best. There just wasn't much.' He slammed a fist into the arm of his chair. 'If we'd had that murder weapon...'

Bennet decided to move on to a detail that had bothered him. He knew it was a tricky item to bring up though. 'I thought you might have seen a connection when I told you that the victims had sawdust forced into their eyes.'

His father gave a slow nod. 'No doubt that is a question that will be brought up when the public learns of this similar old case. Hindsight is a great tool. I'll tell you what I'll tell anyone else who asks. One was sand, one was sawdust, and my case was many years ago. Those cases seem similar now, because of this new double murder, but back then they didn't. If the public had seen a connection between my case and the Ryan murder years later, we would have heard about it because the Ryan detectives would have wanted to see the Davies files. That didn't happen.'

'I didn't mean it as an accusation. I'm sorry. I was just thinking...'

'That we could have made this connection much earlier. I

understand. But now you think there's a definite connection? We're talking about a long time between both cases.'

'Three cases,' Bennet said, and upon the confusion displayed by his father, he launched into an outline of the murder of Holly Ryan at a woodyard in 1979. By its end, his father was breathing fast.

'That's an amazing coincidence, Liam. And, yes, I did use that word on purpose. If there is a connection between these three cases, you cannot be thinking about one murderer. He'd be my age.'

Bennet's phone beeped with a message from Liz. He had to read it twice to be certain his eyes weren't lying.

'What is it, son?'

'They're in the same area. Pond Street and '79, the woodyard. Pond Street basically sits right where Harrison's woodyard was. Liz just made the connection because of an unexploded World War Two bomb being found there in 1948 by a pair of–'

'Twins,' his father cut in. And when Bennet looked up, he saw his father's jaw was dropped, too.

43

Bennet chose a Premier Inn near Meadowhall shopping centre and, with Hollywood timing, turned into the car park just as Liz was exiting her vehicle. Her shorter journey had taken longer not because she'd had to collect her vehicle from outside his house, but due to a stop he'd asked her to make at her station to use a printer.

They'd talked on the phone as each travelled back to Sheffield, so all she said now was, 'Will they mind my being here?'

'They haven't got a choice. And you helped us make a big leap.'

They headed inside, to a room on the first floor that was already booked. The rest of the team was already here, bleary-eyed at five in the morning because they'd been working until past midnight and Bennet had called them at little past 3am. He hadn't divulged anything except to claim there had been a breakthrough of sorts and that he was holding an urgent meeting.

But none are so curious as detectives, so upon his entry into the room they fired a volley of questions. After he'd calmed them down, they noticed Liz's presence. DC Ralph Hooper looked perturbed about that.

The team sat on the two wooden chairs, the two beds, or the floor, and Bennet stood amongst them as if about to impart a campfire story.

'I know we had a briefing planned for ten o'clock, but this couldn't wait. I was speaking to my father just a few hours ago, and DI Miller here was talking with the son of the lead detective from the woodyard murder of Holly Ryan in '79. The reason I spoke to my father is because we've learned that there is a third, perhaps connected case.'

He outlined the Wandle School murder. If there was amazement that a connection involved an investigation by their SIO's father years ago, they didn't show it.

He said, 'Three cases, over fifty years apart. At first glance similar only in method. Throats cut, heads and faces smashed in, and sand or sawdust poured into the eyes. One in a school, 1967, one in a woodyard in 1979, one on a housing estate just yesterday. The locations themselves are unconnected by appearance, style, anything like that. Except for one detail. Time. Liz.'

Liz cleared her throat and stepped up. Ever since Bennet had told her he wanted her to speak before his team, she'd been nervous. At first she'd tried to allay her fears by reminding herself she was a DI and outranked them. It didn't work. In the end, she could only hope that the information mattered, not the storyteller.

She took a rolled stack of six sheets of A4 paper from her pocket and pinned it to the wall. The top one was a photocopy of a Sheffield map. There was a red dot the size of a five-pence piece. She pointed with a pen.

'Yesterday. Eighty-eight Pond Street on the Oakland housing estate. Here's our bodies.' She took a pushpin and pierced the red circle.

She tore away the sheet to expose another beneath. Another map. This one wasn't a Google photograph, it was black and white and had NOT FOR COMMERCIAL REUSE stamped all over it.

'This is an historical map from 1977, two years before the Holly Ryan murder.' She tapped the pin. Here, the housing estate was gone. In its place was Harrison's Timber Merchant. She heard the team give excited whisperings.

'The exact same spot. The woodyard was demolished in the late eighties and by 1991, the new housing estate was up. But it gets better.'

She ripped the sheet away, leaving the pin remaining in a third A4 sheet. An older picture, again marked as not for commercial reuse. Same website. No woodyard here. It was marked 1964. Now, like a giant 3D flagpole, the pin stuck out of a different sprawl of buildings.

Wandle School.

'In 1948 an unexploded bomb was discovered in Wandle School, under a boys' toilet cubicle. DCI Bennet's father remembers a sense of nervousness about this from his men as they searched the old school following the murder of Harold Davies in '67. A similar nervousness, about treading around an old bomb site, was felt by murder detectives investigating the Holly Ryan killing in '79. It was this that led us to realise both crimes were committed on the exact same spot. Fortunately, the media hasn't yet made the connection. But there's more.'

The team started murmuring. Liz took a second to compose herself. It was easy: nobody looked bored yet.

Everybody fell silent when Liz tore away sheet three. On sheet four was an overhead photograph of Harrison's woodyard. It showed a tented crime scene, with police around it. North was a retaining fence alongside the river. She moved the pin, and jabbed it into the tent, which was about the size of a pound coin on the photo. She then jabbed a second pin into the river, directly above the first pin, and into what Liz had thought of as the bone-pipe that crossed the water.

When she ripped away this sheet, it exposed a photograph of the same location, from the same height and same angle. But the terrain had changed again. The second pin was still in the bone-pipe, which was now located in a barren patch of land. But the first pin was in number 88 Pond Street.

Then she ripped away this sheet to expose the final one: a floor plan of the house. The first pin was in the kitchen. A specific part of the kitchen.

Bennet stepped up to calm his suddenly lively team. 'We can now forget about getting into the Lawlers' lives to see why their house was picked. They're not involved. They know nothing. It's all about their house. And it wasn't picked because it looked easy to break into or because they were away on holiday. It all centres around that very spot right there, which was where the Lawlers' brand-new fridge-freezer sat. Our killer moved the freezer so that he could place the two bodies into that space, but not to hide them. It was because that was *exactly* where the body of Holly Ryan was found forty years earlier.'

44

———

Bennet had outlined all the potential scenarios they were facing, and allowed his team to debate each one. Some held no water with anyone, like the idea of one killer responsible for all three crimes. If the killer of Harold Davies at Wandle School in '67 had also slaughtered the pair at Pond Street, then he would be an old, old man. The female victim at Pond Street was small and petite and the male, Carl Roddis, showed evidence of extreme weight loss and muscle atrophy through starvation. Both were incapacitated by a heavy amount of isopropyl alcohol. Even so, it was a reach to imagine a pensioner had manhandled and caused such damage to two victims.

Also in doubt was the theory of three separate killers – a random murder at Wandle School in '67, a copycat at the wood-yard in '79, and a separate copycat at Pond Street: too bizarre. Holly Ryan had suffered nine strikes by house brick, but this information wasn't reported to the public. The fact that the Pond Street victims had also received nine blows apiece suggested a link that was more than just the work of a copycat.

And finally, they discarded the notion that there were two killers – that one man had committed the murders in '67 and '79, and a new killer had wreaked carnage at Pond Street. From his father, Bennet had learned that Harold Davies had had his throat cut twice and suffered a single head injury. There was no hand injury. And, perhaps most telling, sand instead of sawdust had been thrust into his eyes. The strong differences between the school and the timber yard crimes hinted that the oldest case was nothing but a recipe. It had certainly been at least loosely copied, but it was a stretch to see anything deeper than that.

That left one scenario: an active killer who'd claimed victims within the last couple of days and forty years ago, and had based his crimes on some old, forgotten murder whose perpetrator was probably dead. This was a notion various detectives in the room found digestible.

Someone said, 'It's only a forty-year gap between Ryan at the timber yard and Pond Street. A teenager would only be in his fifties now. I'm in my fifties and fit as a fiddle. And those two were very similar. I agree.'

Someone else offered, 'If the killer of Ryan tried to copy Wandle in '67 and mistakenly used sawdust at the Ryan killing, he might have chosen sawdust at Pond Street because he wanted to copy his original crime. Perhaps he feels an energy emanating from the location and just because it's now a housing estate, with people living there, that wouldn't stop him.'

Here, Bennet decided to bring Liz back in. Since sharing her information about the brick strikes, she'd remained quiet. He wanted her to feel like part of the team. He asked her to share her thoughts.

When she spoke, it was minus the nerves he'd expected from her, addressing a team that she felt didn't want her here. And she went against what they'd already briefly discussed.

'I think we don't know anything. I think everyone here is

confused by the location and the method. And we're not dealing with copycats, despite the lack of motive.'

All eyes were on her.

'Copycats seek headlines. They want the world to think the same killer was responsible so they can feed off the fear and the outcry while remaining anonymous. It's like infamy by proxy. And they plan their killings in advance. Harold Davies was a thirty-something man, so no copycat wishing to replicate that crime would choose a twenty-something prostitute or a couple in their sixties.'

Someone said, 'What about the Yorkshire Ripper? Could our chap in '79 be copying him? Could it have been Peter Sutcliffe himself? He killed a woman in a woodyard. He was moving on to hunting in Sheffield when he was caught. The police have always suspected he did other Yorkshire murders.'

A couple of detectives found this theory comical. Someone else said, 'None of the Ripper murders involved sand or sawdust forced into the eyes.'

Liz said, 'The Ripper case does play a kind of part here. But '79 was never connected to the Ripper case. Or the '67 case–'

Bennet jumped in here, eager to defend his father. 'My father's team didn't make the connection between his case and ours because in his, sand was thrust into the eyes, and our killer used sawdust. Blunt-force head injuries and throat-slashing are common murder methods, as we've said. Plus, it was twelve years later and the case was cold. It should have been up to the detectives in '79 to make the connection, not my father years afterwards.'

Liz said, 'Pulling up cold cases way back was not the same as now. There was no HOLMES database. Checking cold cases meant pulling boxes out of a dusty storeroom. It took time. Here's where the Yorkshire Ripper comes in. The country was in the grip of his killing spree and police everywhere were wondering if dead women on their patch, especially prostitutes, were down to him. In 1978, only eighteen or so months before Holly Ryan's murder, the Ripper had killed a lady in a woodyard. Detectives from the Ripper investigation even visited the Ryan incident room, but soon determined that her killing wasn't connected.

'Despite this, when the Ryan investigators looked for similar cases, they had that infamous series of murders in mind and went back only four years, to '75, which was when the Ripper started his reign of terror. This, and the sheer pressure on police across the country to get the Ripper, might have played a part in why there was never a connection made with the '67 murder in the same area. But in their defence, the earlier murder victim had been a man and sand, not sawdust, had been placed in his eyes.'

She looked at Bennet, who gave a slight smile of thanks.

'So what's your theory?' someone said.

'What about a smokescreen?' Liz said. 'A bona fide copycat in '79 would have prepared, and copied the crime to a T. And teased the police about it, to make sure the connection was established. But what about if the killer knew his victim?'

No response. They wanted to hear more.

'Picture him after killing Holly Ryan. He panics. He knows the police will get into the victim's social circle, even though most attacks on prostitutes are by strangers. He'll be questioned. He'll say something silly, and he won't have an alibi, and the police will look at him a little harder, and they'll dig deeper, and he'll go to prison for the rest of his life.

'But he has an idea. He's local, so he knows there was a killing on that spot twelve years ago, when he was just a kid. His plan: copy that crime. Wandle School is now a woodyard, so there's no sand, but there is sawdust. Good enough for his purposes. Good enough to make the police connect the crimes.

Two murders, one killer. Perfect. No matter how guilty he acts, how weak his alibi, the police won't look hard or dig deep. He's too young to be a viable suspect for Wandle. Which in turn rules him out for the murder of Holly Ryan, too.'

She waited for a rebuke, or laughter. She got only questions. 'But what about Pond Street? How does that figure?'

'And it doesn't explain Mark and Vicky Lawler. Why not kill them? Why these other two victims brought in from elsewhere?'

Others tossed their opinions into the mix:

'They were on holiday.'

'Yet he found two victims. Who? A pair of Jehovah's Witnesses or encyclopaedia salesmen who knocked on the wrong door at the wrong time?'

'Or maybe he had two accomplices with him and when they found the Lawlers out, one killed the other two?'

'Could be. The victims in '67 and '79 were different, so age and sex at Pond Street was unimportant.'

'But Holly Ryan was killed on June 23rd, Harold Davies on March 16th, so dates are unimportant. So why not return to Pond Street another night, when the owners were in?'

Myriad chattering voices. Liz waited for a lull. 'If we accept the idea that the murder of Holly Ryan was made to look like a copy in order to divert attention away from the truth, perhaps the same applies today. What if location and method were designed for the police to think there was a connection to old unsolved murders? To direct us away from the part that matters. The victims.'

Bennet had to call for quiet again. 'Liz, am I right in saying you believe there was one thing and one thing only important to our killer? Not the place, or the method of murder. You're saying the killer wanted Carl Roddis and the unknown woman dead.'

45

There was one final piece of business. Bennet said, 'DI Todd, you mentioned on the phone a Twitter trick. Now's the time to elaborate.'

Sienna Todd stood up. She ran through what they knew about Carl Roddis. Born in Sheffield in 1957. Stannington, his original home, was only a little more than a mile from Pond Street to the east. Worked for a printing company and left Sheffield when it downsized. Went to prison for assault on the ex-wife's brother in 2000, when he was forty-three. Vanished in 2016. Post-mortem said he was suffering from long-term malnutrition. No friends or family have heard from him in all that time. And then she got to her news, which concerned his younger brother, Darren, suspected to be living in New York.

'My sister is married to a journalist for *Newsday*, a New York paper that has a circulation of about half a million. I got hold of her and her husband's going to put our murder story in their paper later today and on their Twitter feed in the next few hours. That's another 300,000 followers. The brother, Darren, doesn't have a Twitter account, at least under that name. But there's a chance he'll see it. Even though it's a Sheffield, England murder, they'll list a phone number. The one for Crimestoppers, so our incident room doesn't get inundated with a whole fresh new bunch of cranks from overseas.'

The meeting ended after Liz had handed out flash drives containing all the files that Xander Jackson had given her. The team dispersed, but Bennet and Liz were so tired that they decided to sleep a couple of hours. The last to leave was Hooper. Even though Bennet was slumped in a chair and Liz sat on the bed, Hooper gave a sly look back as he left the room.

'He's going to spread rumours,' she said as she opened her laptop.

Bennet didn't look up from a file. 'Who?'

'DC Hooper.'

'About what?'

'Us.'

Now he looked up. 'I'll put him on stolen handbags if he does. Anyway, nothing is going to happen.'

'Oh, because it's your choice, is it?'

His embarrassment made her laugh. She showed her ring finger. 'Remember, I wear this to keep men away. Not interested.'

'I think you wear that for another reason. The same reason you don't wear makeup.'

She stopped smiling. 'Oh. What are you, a detective and a psychologist? And I do wear makeup sometimes.'

'Yes, you do, and I've not quite worked that out yet.'

'Well, enlighten me when you do.'

He said nothing further on the subject and she concentrated on her computer, trying hard to shift her attention. Holly, Holly, Holly. At first it was hard and she kept glancing at Bennet, but he had his eyes closed. Then, the more she read, the easier it got to become sucked into history.

She wondered about the discarded clothing of Holly Ryan. It was the only aspect of that case that kept haunting her, deflecting her from Pond Street. She'd always felt that Pond Street would be solved or not without her input and more focus was needed on Holly's murder. But she knew she was fooling herself. This was more of what everyone had always thought about her: that she loved the glory of solving a case. Not for justice, or to bring peace to satellite victims, but for her own pride, for praise.

Before, she'd hated that theory. But it was becoming harder to deny. She knew how good it would look if she either solved the Ryan case or found something about that murder that contributed to success with Pond Street. But how much of it was plain and simple limelight, and how much was a desire to prove to everyone, her sister included, that she was good at her job?

Her eyes started to droop as she flicked through statements, handwritten theories by the lead detective, Jackson, and crime-scene photos. Two photos had previously intrigued her, one especially so.

She heard a thud. Bennet had leaned to one side in his chair and files had slid off his lap, onto the floor. He was asleep, but slightly overbalanced.

Holly Ryan's high heels had been thrown over a wooden fence just metres from where she lay, into a watery ditch that couldn't be observed from the crime scene. To the north of her body. But her fluffy teddy fur coat had been stuffed under a water tank to the south.

Something seemed wrong about this because it meant the killer, after moving one way to dump her shoes, had then taken off her coat and travelled in the other direction to hide it. There had been various better places to hide evidence. And it hadn't really been hidden. Although the low ground clearance of the water tank – seven or eight inches – meant no room for someone to clamber under, the coat had been visible from anywhere more than about three metres away. Police had spotted it from the crime scene and pulled it out with a stick.

Something bothered her about that hiding place for the coat. But she didn't know why.

She heard another series of thuds as the remaining files on Bennet's lap tumbled to the carpet. 'Liam,' she called, and he jerked awake in time to stop himself tumbling. 'Lie on the bed. It's fine.'

She shifted to one edge and he took the other, so there was four feet between them. Extra respectful, he placed his files in the space.

'This is Sam Thomas?' he said, reaching out to turn her laptop slightly his way. The photo, a black and white from a newspaper, showed a winner's podium against a backdrop of onlookers, with three men on it, each in riding gear and holding a trophy. Sam Thomas's was the biggest. The third solo tournament win for the Sheffield Falcons' most successful speedway star. He'd been captured giving a smile and a thumbs up. The resolution wasn't clear, but it looked as if he had a scrape or burn on his hand. There was also a tattoo on his neck, but she couldn't make it out. He was handsome and successful enough to surround himself with girls, so it struck her as a puzzle that he'd spend time hanging around prostitutes. Unless he truly was a saint. She read a little more and then heard a wheezy drawl.

He was asleep, she saw. She continued to read even though tiredness was threatening to overcome her too. The next thing she knew, she woke flat on her back with her laptop having slipped off her chest, into her neck. And a weight on her right breast.

Bennet was lying in the middle of the bed, asleep atop the files he'd placed there. One hand was across his face. The other, his left, created the weight on her breast.

She lifted the laptop away and sat up. Bennet's hand slid off and into her lap. She lifted his wrist and placed his arm on the bed. He didn't wake. She got up and tried not to think about how long it had been since anyone had touched her. It had been three weeks since she and Dan had split up.

Not long enough for attraction to another man to stop feeling wrong. She got up and quickly made her exit.

46

‘What we've got is one killer, and two killers, and three killers.’

Superintendent Hunter looked round at Bennet as he tried to jab the number seven. He hit the one above instead, a four, and Polos instead of Quavers dropped into the canteen vending machine's delivery tray. He fished in his pocket for more coins. The super threw the Polos onto the table as he retook his seat.

‘Explain that, Liam. And I hope you don't mean a total of six murderers out there.’

‘My team couldn't agree. I had one, Taylor, say one killer.’

Hunter opened his Quavers with more annoyance than needed, and the bag split and dumped curly yellow crisps on the table. ‘Taylor's got that grandfather who runs those half-marathons, so he's her proof OAPs have the energy. How many said six killers?’

Bennet grinned around a mouthful of lasagne. ‘Six was your joke.’

‘Oh yeah. Three, I mean. How many said three?’

‘Just one. DI Miller.’ Before Hunter could demur, Bennet

added, 'I know, I know. Look, my father knows her super and called him to complain about her.'

'I know. Allenberg complained to me.'

'Well everybody can calm down. She's going back to her own station. Her team recently closed an investigation and she's got a couple of days off. She offered to assist, that's all.'

The super crunched a crisp. 'She just wants her name in the newspapers.'

'If her assistance helps catch our killer, what's the problem? If she's mentioned instead of me, good. I hate the limelight.'

'Well, tell her to work fast because I doubt she's got two days. Her DCI, Bates, is it? The chap in hospital. He's been replaced by DCI Jollops for the interim. Jollops will want to call the team in to get acquainted with them and their cases. He won't want her working Pond Street, even on her days off.'

'I'll send her back today. I'll call her as soon as I leave here.'

The super nodded. 'Anyway, what do you think? One, two or three? Or six? Killers.'

'I lean towards two killers. I think we have one perp for the first two. There was only a twelve-year gap, which means the killer could have been in prison, or suppressing his urges. If Harold Davies in '67 was his first, or his most memorable kill, maybe the scene had something for him. So he went back. Easily done, because Wandle School was a woodyard by then. Bleak, closed at night so pretty desolate. But with Pond Street, it involved breaking into a house somehow. Much harder. That's a different killer, no doubt. Possibly a copycat.'

'Anything connecting the Pond Street victims with the other two yet?'

'Nothing found so far. For Carl Roddis, at least. If there is a connection to Ryan and Davies, it might come from the unidentified female victim. But until we have her name, we won't know. No closer to that.'

'You were compiling a list of inmates Carl Roddis was in Leeds Prison with – in 2000, was it?'

'It was. It's a long list. Murderers are easy to eliminate because they're still locked up. Reoffenders are doing us a favour in that department, too. But some car thief who did six months nearly twenty years ago, and then went straight, is a little harder to trace. We'll get there.'

The super ate another Quaver as he pondered this. 'What about this reference to the number nine?'

Bennet knew he was referring to the number of head strikes upon Holly Ryan and the Pond Street pair. 'Probably nothing. No nines figured in my father's old case as far as we're aware. Coincidence, if anything. We're still looking into it.'

The super sat up straighter. 'On to other matters. The district commander wants to know the pros and cons of alerting the media to the potential connection between the three cases. He's in a meeting about it now and I'll know his answer later today. There could be people out there with vital information. I know you were dead against it because it will increase your workload. Your thoughts now?'

'Tell the commander that the millisecond he connects the cases, it all becomes one major investigation with his name attached. And he'll be blamed when his detectives don't solve a murder that was already frozen solid by the time he left school.'

Superhunter laughed. 'Not in those words, but I did stress that point. Hence why he's delayed.'

'The longer the media don't make the leap, the better. We gave the public the information about the female victim at Pond Street and that's all we need their help with at the minute.'

'Not that they've been much help. What about the Roddis brother? Darren. Has he heard the news and called yet?'

'You know I would have already said. Nothing yet.'

'Heck, maybe he did it.'

'We'll see. You missed one.' Bennet pointed by the super's elbow, where there was an errant Quaver. It was soon chewed and swallowed.

'Can you cope with this one on your plate? As well as your other cases?'

Bennet caught that careful, long look from his boss again. 'Cut to it, sir. What's going on?'

'I see it in your face, Liam. You like this Detective Miller. You feel sorry for her.'

'She's been hounded by rumours, doesn't get the respect she deserves. She made a lot of headway in this case. And as for seeking glory, well, she hasn't let that get in the way of some hard work. What are you getting at?'

'The commander spoke to me about something else. He gave me a choice. Regarding your like of Detective Miller and your hate of fame and glory, I'm going to relay that same choice to you.'

As Liz was getting changed for swimming in her attic room, she got a text from an unknown number, and it didn't waste words: TEAM BRIEFING. RETURN ASAP.

She understood. Her boss, DCI Bates, had been replaced and the new head of Major Investigation Team 2, whoever he was, was recalling the team so he or she could be briefed on current cases. She called Bennet, but he didn't answer. However, he too understood what was going on, because he sent a text a minute later. And this one was even more economical: GO BACK. She called again, but he didn't answer.

'I've got two days off, Liam,' she started her voicemail message. 'I still want to help on this.'

She looked on the clothing rail for a clean suit. There wasn't one. Still wearing her bathing suit, she dashed downstairs clutching the outfit she'd worn overnight, rubbed water on a couple of dirty patches, and ironed it in the kitchen. She gave her face a scrub, too.

As she was putting the ironing board away, she heard the gravelly crunch of a car returning. Gill and her husband Freddie, back from wherever. Knowing she had little time, Liz dragged the outfit on right over her bathing suit. Then, fearing Gill's wrath, she scoured the fridge for out-of-date items and found a ready meal with today's date.

She lobbed it in the bin and left through the back door just as Gill and her husband entered the house. Gill would moan about the unlocked back door, but it beat facing her sister this morning. Liz ran to her car and was away within seconds.

She drove angrily. Bennet had booted her off the case, right when it was getting juicy. The new boss was probably going to put her on boring follow-up tasks on one of their existing cases.

At Woodseats station, she entered the CID office to find her team bustled around one of their incident boards, tacking up pictures and sheets of paper. This bustle could only mean a new murder had come in.

Then she stopped as she spotted a tall, handsome and prematurely grey man in a suit.

'DI Miller, welcome back,' DCI Joshua Jollops said. Her heart sank. 'You're late.'

All the old disdain reared up.

'I'm not late. I just got the call like ten minutes ago.'

'The others got here on time, as you can see. If you hadn't been frolicking about somewhere, you wouldn't have been late.'

She tuned him out as the new incident board caught her attention. She recognised a photograph of a household kitchen, awash in blood. Her legs felt wobbly.

The Pond Street double murder. It was back with her team.

48

L iam and Hooper were standing in their own incident room, just looking for a eureka connection between A and B amongst the various whiteboards and myriad sheets of paper and photographs white-tacked up. Enquiry officers were out rapping on doors while the remainder of the team were in the files and on the phones. A different case, with different evidence and scenes and witnesses, but the murder room operated the same as always.

'Shame about Pond Street,' Hooper said. 'We might have closed it in a day or two.'

'It was a pain in the backside. The Lawlers are kicking up a stink in the papers because their house hasn't been released back to them yet. I'm glad to be out of it.'

'But we were so close.'

'As long as the bad guy is caught.'

'You truthfully don't mind having to give it up? We haven't handed over all the files and stuff yet. Not too late to request it stays with us.'

Bennet shook his head. 'It was too high-profile for my tastes.'

'Remember, if this killer thinks he's the god Thor and it turns out he used a hammer to crush their heads, I said it first.'

Bennet managed a smile. After his chat with Liz about the relevance of the number nine – the amount of head strikes to Holly Ryan and the Pond Street victims – Bennet had mentioned it to members of his team. He'd had all sorts of texts about Chinese medicine, Indian culture, the Aztecs, and religion. Hooper's input had been Norse mythology. Nine worlds, and nine steps by Thor, or whatever.

'At ease, Ralph. I'll make sure DCI Jollops mentions your name at the press conference.'

'Good man. You know, I'm surprised the super passed the case on. It might look a little like he couldn't handle it. And Miller won't be too happy being under Jollops. Under him in a different way, this time.'

Bennet said nothing, but he gave a quizzical look.

'You didn't know they have a history?' Hooper said. 'Climbing the slimy pole. Literally.'

So, Jollops was the colleague she'd had a relationship with. He tried not to care. 'Give her a break.'

'I will. He won't. Bet he's pissed at her. Exes always are.'

'Jollops is a seasoned pro. He won't let their history get in the way.'

'We'll see. If he gives her something meaty – no pun – then he's fine. If he's got her, I don't know, redoing the house-to-house or something, then we'll know he's pissed.'

'Leave it, Ralph.'

They were silent for a moment, and then Hooper said, 'Sir, I know you're waiting to do this. But I'll bring it up. I know I made a mistake delaying the fingerprints on the Pond Street victims. And although you haven't mentioned it, I know it was also a mistake that I didn't find out about the Wandle School murder earlier. I know we looked for similar cases before that phone call from Charles Hardy about a copycat, but after it I should have made a bigger effort. I don't know. I was just so overwhelmed by that phone call. I...'

'Don't worry about it, Ralph. Those cases were so long ago that many details were omitted when they were inputted on the computers. It's hard to find much about the Wandle School murder. My father didn't immediately make the connection between that and '79 even though I told him about the Ryan murder. It's not your fault. It happens.'

'Well, it won't happen again–'

Both men turned as one of the girls on the phones yelled, 'Sir, I have Darren Roddis on the line.'

The whole room watched as Bennet rushed across and seized the phone.

'You're Detective Bennet, right? Not some lackey pretending to be?'

'It's me. Where are you, sir?'

'New York. I saw the news about it. A newspaper tweet, of all things. That's how I find out my brother is dead. What happened? And is it definitely him?'

'It's him. Mr Roddis, I need to speak with you in person. I can make my way to you, but we wouldn't speak until at least tom–'

'Hell no, Bennet. I want to know everything that's happened. I want to see things for myself, and I want to see my brother's body. And I'm going to stay by your side until you catch the monster who killed him.'

'You'll need to call me when you have the details of your flight and airline, Mr Roddis, so that–'

'It's not Roddis any longer, and I'll tell you my flight details right now, detective. I'll be on a private Gulfstream IV and I'll be in Sheffield in about eight hours.'

And he hung up.

49

—————

When Bennet rang her, she considered not answering the call. And when she did, she said nothing. He heard a car engine, as if she was driving.

'Liz? You there?'

She said nothing again.

'Liz, I know you just got a shock. You were heading back to your team no matter what. My super offered me a choice, Liz, and I made the one that was best for you. You started on the case, you did the most work. I gave Pond Street back to your team. I did that for you.'

'You did that for me?' Brief surprise didn't dampen her annoyance. 'But I've got nothing. Jollops isn't entirely convinced that all three cases are connected and he's punishing me by giving me a horse-dung-useless-follow-up on the Holly Ryan murder. You know, the forty-year-old cold case?'

He got the scorn in her tone. 'That's not useless, Liz. The cases are connected, remember. Maybe Jollops thought you were the best for the job.'

'No, Liam, he's sticking it to me. Remember I said I had a

relationship with a fellow officer? Well, it was him. Seven years ago, when I was a DC and he was a DS. Didn't end well and now he's getting revenge. Next, I suspect he'll have me off to interview some old friend of Harold Davies from '67.'

'Well, at least he's working on the connections we came up with. I expected him to ignore the two old murders. But think positively, Liz. You're on the case. That was what you wanted. And that's why I'm calling. My name was on the tweet the New York newspaper put out, and I got a call.'

She nearly swerved into oncoming traffic. 'From Darren Roddis?'

'He's rather angry about his brother's death and having to find out through Twitter.'

'Did you mention that that was his fault for vanishing to another country without word?'

'I didn't get a chance. He said he's coming down and hung up. By private jet. Right now.'

'Private jet?'

'The so-called withdrawn freak that his ex-sister-in-law talked about appears to have done well for himself without his brother. He's just sent word that he'll be at Sheffield Aero Club in a few hours.'

Liz checked her watch. 'I want to meet him with you.'

'Good. I was thinking we could do dinner first.'

She remembered how well she and Jollops had gotten on, before that drunken night. And now look. She had left her station because of the awkwardness of working with him, but he was back in her life. She couldn't help but feel that, even though it was just dinner, she might end up regretting it.

'Okay. Dinner,' she said, surprising herself.

'Okay. Great. Look, I'll send a text with the Aero Club address and what time to meet me there. But tell Jollops about meeting Roddis with me, and don't go behind his back if he says no.'

She hung up without a reply to his request.

50

When the two beautiful phone calls came, Liz was deep into the horse-dung-useless-follow-up at the behest of DCI Jollops. He had put her on hunting down the prostitutes who'd been known to work with Holly around the time she was killed. Of nine prostitutes interviewed in the original investigation, four were dead and one was living overseas. One other had refused to speak to her because that old life of hers belonged to another world. Two others had seemingly dropped off the face of the earth.

The single one she'd traced, a lady called Petra, had agreed to meet with her, but it had been a waste of time. Even back in '79, Petra had had a memory shot to hell because of – she claimed – brain damage due to a violent pimp. Lovely. Liz hadn't been hopeful that the woman would suddenly remember something new from forty years ago, but Jollops had insisted that she made the visit.

Amazingly, the woman had still been on the game at sixty-three years of age, but now her cover was as a masseuse. The giveaway was that lubricant had been nestled in amongst her massage oils, and the massage table was a bed. And she had had no problem being interviewed right there in that upstairs room in her flat in Ecclesall. She'd sat on the bed and suggested Liz do the same. She'd offered to rub Liz's shoulders while they talked. The woman was keen to help and answered every question – without question.

But Petra the Prostitute hadn't been able to supply any new evidence, hadn't known about Holly's womb cancer, and hadn't heard for two days about Holly's death. She had met Sam Thomas, the local speedway star who'd been good friends with Holly Ryan and was once a suspect in her slaughter. She'd confirmed that he was saint-like to the girls, with gifts and medicines, maths and English lessons, and that many of the girls had felt the police had had no business even wondering if he was a monstrous killer.

Now, Liz entered the incident room at Woodseats with aching feet, tense shoulders and an utter sense of wasted time. The room was empty of life except for a few staff electronically chasing this or that lead. Jollops was an old-fashioned detective who thought boots on the ground got the best results, preferring his staff to knock on doors and chat face to face. The officers he'd stuck in the office were probably his least favourites.

But they were working the Pond Street murders. He'd sent his absolute least favourite, Liz, on a decomposed line of enquiry in a stone-dead case.

'Where is everyone?' Liz asked the room.

A pretty detective constable on the phone held up a finger, finished the call she was on, and hung up. While typing notes to file, she said, 'DCI Jollops took them to the Blue Swan for a briefing.'

'Instead of here?'

The phone rang again. 'To "jolly them up", as he put it,' the constable said, then answered the call.

'Actually, no, just to piss me off.'

Liz headed for the incident board that displayed the details of all their information on the '79 murder of Holly Ryan. Under the name *Petra Allen/prostitute/friend of victim*, she wrote in wipeable marker: NO FURTHER INFORMATION. That done, it was time to return to her desk, to chase up another old prostitute. But first, tea.

The first beautiful call came as she was watching the old kettle boil and vibrate on the counter. It was from Xander Jackson, son of the lead investigator in Holly Ryan's murder. Without even saying hello, he asked if she wanted to make this a Messenger video call. One glance at her straggly hair in the silver surface of the kettle decided her answer. Hell no.

'Next time, Xander. What have you got for me?'

What he had was a box of files from his attic. Everything from the original case that his father had been able to photocopy. A fraction of the overall mass, but still a bunch. And all Liz had to do was meet him for lunch and it was hers.

'I can't today. Snowed under. But I really need some of that stuff. Can you scan and email what you can? I'd like photographs and the pathologist's report, if you don't mind.'

'Sure thing. Dinner tomorrow?'

'We'll see,' she replied, not sure if she was fobbing him off or not.

'I guess we will.'

After the call, she went to her desk. En route, the second beautiful call arrived. The female constable took it. As Liz was passing her, she heard the young woman say, 'When did your wife go missing, sir?'

Liz moved closer to listen. The constable made attentive noises like *uh-huh* and *mm-hmm* and wrote on a Post-it note. A minute later, the call ended and she started to dial another number.

'What was that about a missing woman?' Liz asked.

The constable said, 'A man in Blackpool called Jack Squires said his wife didn't return last night and didn't turn up for work today. She works at Blackpool Tower. He thought she might have gone to work after staying out with friends, but her work called to say she didn't turn up. He said he saw the thing in the papers and called us. He thinks our nameless woman might be his wife because of that tattoo on her back. I was just going to call DCI Jollops.'

The woman put the phone to her ear. Liz hung it up. 'You've been working the list of inmates who served time with Carl Roddis?'

'Me and Mike, yes. It's tough because it's so long ago.'

'I understand. Look, I'll tell Jollops about the Blackpool call, and I want you to get back on those inmates. I want to change tactic on that a little bit because I've had an idea.'

After explaining, Liz took the Post-it note bearing a phone number and left the incident room. Outside, she received an email. Xander had sent her the pathologist's report on Holly Ryan. She rushed to her car and opened the attachment once cocooned inside. Its contents astounded her.

51

———

'**D**CI Jollops.'

His voice grated on her, as did the sounds of pub life behind him. She could recognise some of her team's voices, and the laughter in the background didn't suggest they were all hard at work. 'It's Liz. I just heard back from a contact with some details about the Ryan murder.'

'The prostitute?'

'No. Xander Jackson, the son of the lead detective. He sent me some files. I found something in the pathologist's report.'

'And what about the prostitute? That was your job, Miller.'

God, now he was referring to her simply by surname. 'That was a bust. She didn't know anything new.'

She heard him slurp a drink, probably a pint of Worthington's. She hated that she remembered his favourite drink. 'Then move on to the next.'

'I am. But I found something good and I've highlighted it. I'll email it over.'

He hung up, the sod. She drove on. He called back four minutes later, angry.

'Miller, what is this crap? This doesn't help us.'

'It's relevant. More relevant than talking to some prostitute with a bad memory. The victims at Pond–'

'Stop, Miller. No more mistakes. I want–'

'We both know I can make a big mistake.' Immediately, she regretted the insult and prayed it would skip over his head, but his long silence said otherwise.

'Miller, there's a chance some of Harold Davies' old boxing club cronies might remember something new. That's next for you. Interview them.'

And with that he hung up. She was raging.

She called Bennet, certain that he'd be more intrigued by what she'd found. 'Liam, I just found something out from the autopsy report on Holly Ryan. She had damage to her left hand, just like the Pond Street duo. Same hand.'

It took him a few ticks to find his words. 'Er, okay. Did you tell Jollops?'

'Yes, and he didn't care. The pathologist recorded all features of Holly Ryan's corpse during his external examination, including birthmarks and tattoos and other marks. On the back of her left hand were four scratches that he said were consistent with fingernails. Light marks, no bleeding, and his diagnosis was that Holly caused the scratches herself. They weren't considered part of the attack on her, which is why the police never paid them any worth, considering the excessive damage to other parts of her body. But we can't ignore them, Liam. The back of the same hand.'

'I understand. But the Pond Street victims didn't have their hands scratched. They were torn up. And if Holly inflicted them herself...'

She felt her heart drop. Jollops she had expected to throw this back in her face, but not Bennet. Or was she wrong? Was she trying to find a link where there wasn't one?

Her foot slipped off the accelerator as she realised she was travelling down the motorway at ninety miles an hour. Like a physical indicator of her desperation to find the solution to this whole thing. She'd thought the urge to reap the glory in this case had left her, but the turmoil she felt at being stifled by her boss and then by Bennet suggested otherwise. Or was it something else? A desire to show Bennet she was good at her job? Prove Jollops wrong?

'A man called about his missing ex-wife,' she said, now eager to convince Bennet that she had something more concrete, that she wasn't running wild. 'With luck, it's our dead female. I'm driving to Blackpool to talk to him and get his wife's DNA.'

But his tone didn't perk up. 'That's good, Liz. Good.'

'What's wrong?'

'I'm not on this investigation anymore, remember? It's nice that you're trying to include me, but Jollops is now the man in charge. Does he know you're driving to Blackpool?'

'But you're meeting Roddis tonight.'

'I know, but he's insisted he wants to talk to me, and I'm taking along a member of the investigating team. You. I'll be passing all my information on. I don't like you keeping things from your boss.'

He didn't believe that Jollops was keeping her out of the investigation, so he wouldn't understand why she was doing this alone. Hell, did she understand it herself?

Spiralling into confusion and despair, she said, 'You're right. I'll tell Jollops right now, and I'll ask him to join us tonight when we meet Roddis,' and hung up before he could reply.

She got as far as hovering her finger over Jollops' name in her recent calls list, then remembered his scathing response the last time she'd called him.

She put the phone away.

52

———

The bed and breakfast was on Palatine Road in central Blackpool, right next door to another one. The sixty-something man behind reception looked up from his crossword puzzle as she entered. He immediately looked a little worried, which puzzled her until she realised her warrant card was hanging around her neck.

'Is this about Linda?'

But before she could answer, he indicated she should follow him with a jerk of his head. He didn't say another word until they'd passed through a door at the end of a STAFF ONLY hallway. It was clear from the size that downstairs was reserved for the owners' residence. They were in a spacious sitting room with two open doors leading to a kitchen and a bedroom.

The owner said, 'You'll want to know how I know it's my wife. Your public appeal didn't show a picture, but it said she had a tattoo of a straight line on her lower back. Linda's got one. From about ten years ago. She wanted to get a picture, but backed out after I'd done just a line. I used to do some tattoos. I just know it's her. I'll get you a picture of her. I know you can match it to skull shape or whatever you do.'

He turned and left the room. Instead of waiting, she followed him. In the bedroom, she saw two single beds pushed together, but with separate quilts.

'Were you and your wife having marriage problems?'

He was reaching for a picture on a shelf that showed a woman in a bikini on a beach, but stopped and spun on her. 'You said *were*. Why would you say that? You know it's her, don't you? The dead woman you found. It's my Linda. You know it.'

'No. I don't know why I said that. I'm sorry. Is that Linda?'

She stepped up and took the framed photo. The woman was about sixty, which fit, and fake blonde and curly, which fit also. But she had a face, which didn't.

'We couldn't separate. Too old for that singles foolishness. So we tolerated each other. And we had this place. Although it doesn't do that well, so Linda did some days at Blackpool Tower on reception.' His face creased. 'Oh God, now I'm doing it, doing the past-tense thing. It's her, isn't it? That's why a detective came, not uniformed people. Not Lancashire police.'

'We don't know yet, Mr Squires.'

'You'll need this.' From his pocket came a small, clear plastic freezer bag with a toothbrush inside. 'For my wife's DNA. I'm assuming a toothbrush is the best thing to use. I know, if it's her, you'll have to come back. Talk to all her friends. Search this house. Victimology, that's the term, isn't it? You'll have to look into Linda's life, to see if there are clues as to who killed her.'

'It's too early to be talking like that. Let me test this first.' She made sure the bag was sealed, and put it in her pocket. Her eyes had a roam for anything else noteworthy, but nothing flagged. 'Let's go back to the living room and you can tell me what happened.'

Once they were seated, he stared at the window. 'She stays out at night sometimes. At friends' houses. It's weird, how it all goes full circle. We knew each other from our twenties. We got some new friends up here, and had a great time. Then they started to marry off and have children, and the social life falters, doesn't it? Then wives and husbands die, or marriages die, and you find yourself hanging around with your friends again, like you did years back.'

Not quite, Liz thought. Her career had stifled a social life and in the five years she'd been with Dan, she'd never gotten close to any of his friends. Like Dan, they were all at least a decade younger, the boys brash, the girls fairy-headed, none of them her cup of tea.

Splitting from Dan had made her realise how alone she was in the world. Her sister's friends were a nicer bunch, but she kept them at a distance because they could report back to Gill. Besides, she had alienated some of them at the embarrassing dinner party a few days ago when she'd gotten drunk and launched into a lecture about the glories of murder detection. It seemed the only people she truly got up close to these days were rapists and killers.

'You okay?'

Mr Squires was looking at her with a frown. She shook off irrelevant meanderings. 'On the phone you said she went out on the evening before the murders in Sheffield.'

'Two days before. She stayed out overnight. The next day she didn't come back and I didn't think anything of it. She wasn't at work that day, so I thought she was having a day out with friends. But the next day she didn't return, and then I saw that public appeal, where the police were asking for people to report blonde women they hadn't seen for a day and were worried about. But I wasn't worried. Linda did that sort of thing. Even after another day and night, I didn't worry. We both stay away at times. Friends' houses. But then this morning her work called. She hadn't turned up. Linda would never just not turn up for work. I knew then something was wrong. I called her friends, and they hadn't seen her. I remembered that public appeal. And I called you.'

'Have you any idea why she would have gone to Sheffield?'

'Friends, I would say. She was from Sheffield.'

That was an interesting snippet of information. 'Born there? Lived there at one point?'

'She was born there, yes. She lived there until her work made her redundant. She was on holiday down here with friends when I met her. On the beach. My parents were running this place, and she said she'd stay a day. Then another. She just never went back, except to pack.'

'Where did she live in Sheffield? And when did she leave that city?'

His answer sent her rushing to her car, texting Bennet on the way.

53

———

In the car, Jollops called. 'Where are you, DI Miller? I just got told we had a call about the unidentified female victim at–'

'Yes,' she cut in, having been waiting for this. 'You and the others were busy at the pub, so I ran with it. I'm on my way back.'

'You already had a task, Miller.'

'I completed it and didn't want to twiddle my thumbs.'

'Oh yes, completed. I just saw your note about the witness you interviewed. No further information? You must not have asked the right questions. You might have to go back. In fact, you will.'

'She knew nothing more, Mr Jollops. They were street-walking acquaintances forty years ago, that's all. Go interview her yourself if you want. But I found some other information out. I believe the female victim at Pond Street is called Linda Squires. I have DNA to make sure. But I found a connection between Linda Squires and the male victim, Carl Roddis.'

She waited for another rebuke, but curiosity was a powerful emotion. 'Let's have it.'

'Linda was born and bred in Sheffield. She moved to Blackpool in 1982 when she was twenty-two. In Sheffield she worked at a printers–'

He groaned. 'That's it? Sheffield is a major city. Printing is a big industry. Just because Squires and Carl Roddis worked in the same field, it doesn't make a connection.'

'They both lived in Stannington, which narrows it right down. Roddis worked at Taylor and Sons. Squires worked at Fletchers. Those two firms merged in 1980. I'd say the odds are good they knew each other. I looked into the new firm. Taylor-Fletchers has moved offices since and still exists. The manager has been running the place since it started and I called him. He's willing to talk to me. I'm heading back to Sheffield now.'

'Good work, I guess.' An unexpected compliment, but Jollops was soon back on form: 'However, you went off without telling me. I'm not happy about that. Give me the details and I'll put someone else on interviewing the print manager. I've got another job for you. I don't know how, but an old chap who used to box at the gym where Harold Davies trained knows the case is under the microscope again and he's willing to be interviewed again. I want you on that. Call Brodowski about it, she's got the details. But first, Holly Ryan's sister, Elaine Jessop. Packer was going to interview her, but I want a woman on it instead. So I want you there. Go chat to her and see if there's anything new she's remembered.'

She hung up the phone without a word. That sod was determined to keep her side-lined. Well, he wouldn't. It wasn't normally a good idea to interview by phone, because lying was harder to detect, but she had no time. She had to get to him first.

54

Darren Roddis's pilot made all bar one of the necessary permission arrangements for landing at Sheffield Aero Club in Netherthorpe. That one was a ten-pound landing fee, which Bennett paid in cash to an instructor who drove out to aid the Gulfstream IV's touchdown by handheld radio. Bennet waited by his car on the grass by the threshold of runway 36. As he did, he got a text from Liz.

'It's free for short-term parking,' the instructor said upon arrival, as they watched the business jet approach from the west. 'If you need longer, we'll arrange prices.'

Bennet took a last look at Liz's message. 'He'll need longer.'

The jet was a sleek thing that made him jealous. The price tag of sixty thousand for a two-night return trip didn't have the same impact as seeing the aircraft soar in and touch down. He stayed by his car as Roddis exited, unwilling to come across like a servant awaiting a master.

Roddis was tall, a little chubby. He wore a suit under a long coat, like a visiting president or CEO, but atop it all was a baseball cap. Even from fifteen feet out, Bennet could see that the man wore a facial prosthetic on his right cheek and chin: the colour didn't quite match the man's skin tone, maybe because he'd tanned a little since acquiring it. Bennet stuck out his hand. Roddis ignored it.

'I looked into you, Detective Bennet. Your police career is impressive, but I was more surprised to learn you have a BSc in mathematics and statistics from Imperial College London. With such a brain applied to business, you could have made millions.'

'Your research is good. You could have been a detective. Instead, you settled in New York and were educated at North-western University Prosthetics-Orthotics Centre. You studied prosthetics, in part to work on building a career and in part to develop new techniques in order to fix your own face. Now you run Prosthetics Around You, with a flash Manhattan facility and a multi-million-dollar turnover. You're Board Certified, member of the New York State Chapter of American Academy of Ortho-tists and Prosthetists, amongst others. And you have a private jet.'

'All correct apart from the horse crap about serving myself.' He touched his facial prosthetic. 'I know what it's like, obviously. I'm in this to help others. But otherwise your research is good, too. But I already knew you were good. You didn't have to prove it.'

'It was only to prove that your qualifications and your wallet mean nothing to me, sir. You may have come here to get answers, and I will give them. But I agreed to meet you so I can interview you. I'll answer your questions. But you have to answer mine.'

Roddis nodded. 'I want to know about my brother's murder. Everything. I'll answer your questions afterwards.'

Now Roddis stuck out his hand, and Bennet took it.

55

She was ready for the call from Jollops. 'I was just about to call you, sir. I have some new information. The print manager told me that the merger between the two print firms where Squires and Roddis worked was official in 1980, but it was announced to the staff nine months earlier. The brass decided to throw a party at a nightclub called Maximus so the two work-forces could meet and mingle. You'll never guess the date of that party. And where it was.'

Jollops made no guess. 'I just called DCI Bennet from MIT 3 about a little matter. He asked me if I was accompanying you to meet Darren Roddis with him. He was taken aback that I knew nothing about it. But you know about that meeting, don't you? He told you to tell me. Why didn't you?'

'I forgot.'

'This just won't do, Detective Miller. Or the fact that you called the print manager before I could send someone to talk to him. I'm not happy with your conduct and I'll be mentioning it to Superintendent Allenberg sometime soon. You won't be at that meeting tonight when Roddis lands. DCI Bennet is going ahead without you. I want you to interview Holly Ryan's sister and then go home. Understand?'

'Yes. I'm heading there now.'

'Good. Now, what was the information about the merger party?'

What she told him elicited a satisfied grunt. 'Also good work, detective, surprisingly. That opens a new line for us. I'll need you to get hold of all the names of people who worked at those two print firms and attended that party, and question whoever is still alive.'

He hung up. She put her phone away and glanced again at the slip of paper she'd scrawled the merger party data on. Information she'd already passed to Bennet by text.

Maximus nightclub had been on Henney Road, less than a hundred metres from Harrison's Timber Merchant; people often used the woodyard as a shortcut to that thoroughfare. And the merger party was on June 23rd, 1979. The night that Holly Ryan was slaughtered in that woodyard.

PART IV

56

———

The drive was ten miles, twenty minutes. Darren Roddis avoided the nasty subject at first and spoke about his prosthetics work. Bennet said little, waiting. When Darren clammed up and his hands fidgeted, the detective knew the question was coming.

'So, I want to know everything you know about my brother's murder.'

'In the year 2000, the government started the DNA Expansion Programme. They wanted more DNA profiles on the database, so they started to take samples from convicted criminals in prisons.'

Darren looked bewildered. As planned. 'Are we having the same conversation? What's that fun fact got to do with my brother?'

'Your brother was locked up for part of 2000. But the programme didn't get around to Leeds Prison, which is where he was, until 2004. Carl had been a free man for a long time by then. We've got his DNA now, because of his tragic murder. What we don't have is anything of his to match it to yet. Hey, do you recognise where we are yet?'

Darren instinctively glanced out the window. It caused a double-take. 'This is Stannington. Where I used to live. Stannington Road. I remember it. Is the police station here? I thought you said you were based in Barnsley.'

Bennet cut a turn down a side street off Stannington Road, heading south. It was a cul-de-sac that ended at a turning circle surrounding a small green. He parked on the far side of the circle, by a turnstile leading into a dark field.

'So are we not going to the police station?'

Bennet cut the engine. 'Recognise this area?'

Darren gazed out his window into the gloom beyond the turnstile. 'Yes. There was a fence here, and allotments. People used it as a shortcut to the city centre. A long time ago. Look, what did you mean about my brother's DNA? Match it to what? I thought you got his identity by his fingerprints. Why do you need to check his DNA?'

'Oh, and we'll need yours as well for a match. But what we need to match it to is proving hard to find. And yes, like you say, this area was a common walking shortcut south-east to the city centre a mile away. You could still use it as one, but it's tricky because a lot of the land has changed beyond the field.'

The look Darren gave Bennet made it clear he knew the detective was deliberately avoiding the question. He grew concerned. 'What's going on, Detective Bennet. Why are we here? What's this about matching DNA?'

'Let's take a walk.'

'A walk? Why? What's in the field? Wait a minute... My God, are you saying this is where my brother was killed?'

'We'll get to that. Come on. What I want to show you is a bit further.'

Bennet got out, came around and opened Darren's door. The wealthy businessman didn't move at first, but Bennet watched and waited. 'Don't worry about cow dung. It's December, they're all inside.'

Darren pulled his collar tight against the cold and stepped out. Bennet waved an arm, indicating that Darren should go first.

As they started walking through the ploughed field, towards a chain-link fence barely visible at the end, Bennet said, 'Do you remember using this route as a shortcut way back?'

'Yes. A few times. Why?'

'How about in June '79?'

Darren stopped. Bennet had to give his arm a little tug. 'Come on. A bit further.'

They walked. The darkness surrounded them as the street lights from the cul-de-sac fell far behind. The ploughed section ended and their feet pounded patchy grass and hard soil. 'So, is this the route you took when you met Linda Squires?'

'Who?'

'Linda Squires. The young lady you and your brother met on your way to the Maximus nightclub, back on June 23rd, 1979.'

Darren stopped. Bennet had to give his arm another tug. 'A bit further. Come on.'

Once Darren was walking again, Bennet said, 'It was a celebration of sorts. A night at a club to toast the merger of the print firm where your brother worked, and the one where Linda Squires worked. She lived in Stannington, too. More to the east of here. I bet you all bumped into each other back at the edge of this field, just by chance, and got talking and realised you were all headed to the same place. So you went together.'

Darren gave a slow nod, but it was a few seconds before he spoke. 'Yes. Carl and Linda were happy to learn that they would be working together and lived so close to each other. But I didn't know her surname was Squires. She only introduced herself as Linda.'

At the end of the field was a concrete path alongside the chain-link fence. This close, they could see a waste ground beyond the barrier.

'What are you bringing me here to show me? There's nothing here.'

'A little further,' Bennet said. They had reached the path. Darren looked left and right along the path. Then through the fence.

'In that waste ground? That was where he was killed? Answer me.'

'Soon.'

A little to their left there was a missing segment of chain-link. Once through, they walked along rough ground and pushed through periodic waist-high vegetation.

'What are you trying to show me, detective? I don't like this. This isn't where my brother was killed.'

'Not here. A bit further.'

Ahead was a narrow river. They stopped before it. There was a pipe that ran from one bank, over the water, and stabbed deep into the other, like an exposed bone in flesh.

'Right here where we stand used to be Anders Road, on an industrial estate. Behind us were some allotments. Left led out, but to the right was a dead-end, although there was a path you could use. Right here in front of this river was a fence and a gate that said, Harrison's Timber Merchant. You remember it?'

'Not really. Look, detective–'

'So right here, on Anders Road, is where I'm thinking you met her.'

'Linda?'

Bennet offered a cynical smile. 'No, no, you'd already hooked up with her, remember? Then all three of you came this way. A shortcut to the nightclub. And this was where you met a prostitute called Holly Ryan.'

57

Holly Ryan's twin was a sight to behold. Liz had spent a lot of time analysing old pictures of Holly and her savaged body, and right before her was the embodiment of how the dead woman would look today. If she'd avoided someone's bloodlust over forty years ago. It was hypnotic.

It wasn't missed on Elaine Jessop, who stood in the doorway and said, 'I got that same look often way back. I was even used in a police reconstruction of the night Holly died. All those times I berated my sister for her slutty clothing and overdone makeup, and then I wore the same stuff and walked about on the streets just like her. Please, come in.'

They spoke in the kitchen, where Elaine Jessop stood at the sink and gazed out the window at a man her age who was tending to flowers. 'That's my husband. You can't speak to him, okay? He knows not to bring Holly up in front of me. I don't like to talk about it. She's a part of history now and I get on better knowing that. And he won't talk to you about her. So be quick with your questions and be out of here, please. But I will warn you that I've had no eureka moments. Nothing I know is any different to all those years ago. If anything, I remember less today.'

Liz was forced to stand behind Elaine, unable to see the older woman's face. That was something that, as a police officer, she didn't like.

'Holly left home at fifteen, didn't she? This was in early 1971. Why did she leave? Was it the pregnancy?'

Elaine ran water, as if to wash pots. There was only a single teacup, which she held under the tap. 'If you know about that pregnancy, then you know that was why she left. It was what I told the police, but I wasn't certain. Holly had been sleeping around, even though we were only fifteen. In fact, it was February and we'd only just had our birthday the week before, so Holly had been having sex at fourteen. She told me about a boy and she said he'd slipped the condom off just as he was about to... do the deed. She didn't know until it was too late. She'd slept with him only two weeks earlier, but she suspected she was pregnant. I doubted it, but my father overheard the conversation in our bedroom, and he went ballistic. He told her to get out. He said she could go stay with the boy. There was no talking father round once he'd made his mind up. And she was gone by the next morning.'

'But she didn't stay with the boy?'

Elaine had filled the cup with warm water, and now tipped it out and refilled it. It was just nervous playing. 'No. She'd already said she didn't know who he was. Just a boy from a group hanging around outside Redgates, the toy shop on The Moor. That's gone now, that building. They demolished it last year.'

'There are conflicting statements in the files. In June of '79, after her murder, you told police that Holly miscarried. But in a follow-up in '82, you said she'd aborted the child.'

Elaine dropped the cup, loudly, and slapped the tap off. She didn't turn from the sink, still fixated on her sliver of the outside world. 'If you paid attention when you read those old files, you'd know my answer to that. I was in Sheffield centre one day in mid-1972 when I saw her. I was in Atkinson's to return one of their new coats from Afghanistan, because it just stank so badly for some reason. And she was walking past outside. I ran out. We spoke for just a few minutes and then she said she had to go. Despite being my sister, she didn't seem to want to see me. Perhaps she was scared Mum and Dad were about to come out of the shop, too. But there was no child with her. I hadn't seen her since that night she left home, over a year before. She didn't write, or phone, or visit. If she hadn't been pregnant, she would have returned home. There is no shame in being wrong about being pregnant.'

Liz waited, sensing more was due.

'But she didn't return home, did she? And so I became convinced she must have been pregnant, but had miscarried. I don't know why, but I needed to know. In the weeks after her murder, I searched. But hospitals do not keep records forever, and even if the records of a death had been kept because it had only been eight years, sometimes things get lost. I searched funeral homes, too, but in that time three local ones had closed and their records were gone. I searched everywhere. But I didn't get a definitive answer, and so that always left the possibility of a miscarriage open.'

'Did you search cemetery records? The public is allowed access to burial registers.'

'I just told you I searched everywhere, detective. Cemeteries are only required by law to keep records of stillborn babies. Not babies born dead before twenty-eight weeks, as it was back then. Those are just considered to be late miscarriages. Back then it was so different. You didn't get counselling. You weren't involved in the whole process like now. Often parents weren't even told what had happened to their little babies' bodies. Babies were sometimes heaped together in one grave and it was left unmarked except for a plot number in a dusty book down in some forgotten cellar. That's an atrocious law that should change.'

Liz wasn't sure which law Elaine meant, but there was no time for an explanation. 'But then you changed your opinion. By '82 you were convinced Holly had aborted the child.'

'Mum and Dad just seemed to get on with life. I still sort of resent them for that, even though they're both dead now. But I couldn't. My sister was dead and I couldn't have her life mean nothing. I wanted a legacy. I wanted a child to be out there. So again I searched, but in a whole different frame of mind this time.'

Elaine filled the cup again, but this time drank heavily from it. 'Because Holly was a prostitute, I thought she might have had the baby but been forced to give it up and put it into care. They go into care for all sorts of reasons, don't they? Dead parent, parent in prison, whatever. Back in '71, when Holly would have given the baby up, if there was one, there were 87,000 children in care. I remember it. I won't ever forget that number. Less than half were boarded out. Those who didn't get foster parents were in remand homes, or special boarding schools, or children's homes. And those poor ones are three times as likely to die as other children.'

'Horrible numbers, indeed. But if Holly put her baby into care, there would be a birth record, Elaine. There isn't.'

'I knew that at the time, but I prayed that that could be down to a simple error. But there was no record of a child in care, and that was when I finally accepted the only other explanation. Abortion.' She wiped a leaky eye. 'It all made sense. I now think she was scared to face me that day in the shop because she'd destroyed that unborn baby. Mum and Dad were dead against such a thing. They used to talk about it long before Holly said she was pregnant. Holly couldn't face us all after what she'd done. I know it now.'

'But there would be burial or cremation records, and you said–'

'I know what I said.' Elaine took a deep breath. 'This was only a few years after abortion became legal. Before then, back-street abortionists were all over the place. Some of those pathetic people made a living out of it. If a woman didn't want to stick a knitting needle into herself, the only way to lose the baby was to pay these people whatever they wanted. There were still illegal abortionists around, because the new law didn't just mean any woman who didn't want a baby could go ahead and have it slaughtered. These were people with basic medical skills, but because this was what they did, killing babies, they'd been out of work for years and were unlikely to find regular employment. So they carried on, but in back alleys and...'

'You think Holly...'

'I bet it was easy for prostitutes to find these abortionists and I know that's what Holly did. I just know it. And she didn't take the remains to a funeral home. Perhaps she had a private service with just herself. Or the abortionist got rid of the remains. Or Holly tossed them in a bin.'

Cruel words, but the woman was still damaged after all these years. Plainly, it wasn't just her parents who were anti-abortion. 'But you never asked her.'

'How could I? I didn't see her again after that day at the toy shop, not alive. By the time she died, I'd known she was on the game for a long time. I'd heard rumours from neighbours. And the police confirmed it when they told us she was dead. I thought it was why she never contacted us. Embarrassed, that was what I thought. For being a prostitute and for killing that baby.'

She turned to Liz. 'The police didn't put much of an effort in all those years ago when Holly's body was still fresh. She was just a prostitute, wasn't she? The only time anyone seemed to care was when detectives hunting the Yorkshire Ripper came down to see if Holly's murder was one of his. And when it was deemed not to be, the limelight, you might call it, faded.

'When my mother died in '95 and the murder was local news again for five measly minutes, they had a little relook, but nothing came of it. I know they had some DNA, because that was a big new thing by then, but it didn't match anything. After that, she once again became an old, forgotten story. I've heard the rumours, detective. There's been another murder where that old timber place used to be, respectable people this time, and that's why you're here. Nobody is trying to solve Holly's murder. They just want to get more information so they can solve this new one, which matters because the dead people weren't home-less, they weren't prostitutes. So I don't know why you're asking questions about a baby from forty years ago. Please get to some-thing more relevant before my husband comes in.'

'I'm sorry you feel that way. The police did care back then and we care now. Holly's case isn't closed. We never close murder cases.'

Elaine scoffed at that. 'I hope you don't mean to fool me with ideas of an incident room full of people still working on my sister's murder. I know they probably have one snot-nosed constable look through the files once every six months.'

'Elaine, I'm sorry they failed back then. Regardless of what's happened in the past, right now we want nothing more than to solve this. There just isn't much new information after so many years. There's a chance today's technology can achieve a break-through, but otherwise all we can do is look again at the files and reinterview people, and hope that we learn something someone might have missed.'

Elaine faced the window again. 'Well it won't help and you're tearing at healing wounds. Just move on, please.'

Elaine turned back to the window. Liz decided to move on to her next subject, while she had time. 'I'd like to ask you about a man called Sam Thomas. Do you know that name?'

'Yes. He visited me.'

She hadn't expected that. 'He visited you?'

'I only heard his name afterwards, after she died. Rumours again. And the police back then asked the same thing. He was some biker sportsman, wasn't he? Had that bird tattoo on his neck. After the murder, I went to the area where they said she worked, near where she was killed. I spoke to some of the night girls. But they didn't know much. They said Holly wasn't the sort to hang around with them. She was a loner. It made it hard to trace any of her clients who might have been violent. But the women did mention that the police were looking at the sports-man. They were surprised by this though.'

Here, Elaine paused for another drink of water. Liz felt the lady was building to an answer to her question, but she was impatient and pushed: 'You say he visited you?'

'The girls said when it was raining or snowing, this man, Sam Thomas, he would come round with sandwiches. He used to like to bandage their cuts, if they got any, and brush their hair. But he never wanted sex from them. They thought his mum might have been a prostitute and he was trying to help her memory by helping these girls. And, as the files no doubt say, I heard that he sometimes liked to let Holly sleep in a barn on his farm, although he pretended he never knew. For someone willing to help these girls, I don't think that sounds right of him to just let her sleep there and pretend he didn't know. But a lot of the girls said he was like a saint, and that was why most of them never said a bad word to the police about him. A saint? Sounds more like a pimp to me.'

'Tell me about the visit from him. Please.'

'I don't know how he found my address. But he turned up on my doorstep. He looked sad. Pathetic. He said he wished he could have taken Holly's pain away. And he tried to grab me. And he told me about Holly's womb cancer. I didn't know how to feel about that.'

'He tried to grab you? In what way? To hurt you?'

Daze-like, staring into nothing, Elaine seemed not to have heard the question, or ignored it. 'The autopsy confirmed the womb cancer, but until then I refused to believe it. Because it was just some man at my door telling me. It was just words. The womb cancer made us feel better, if I'm honest. Well, Mum and me. Dad seemed just angry, and I think part of that was his good name being smeared because his daughter was a prostitute. It's why he wanted the funeral in Chesterfield, not Sheffield. He didn't want any of the locals to know.'

Liz was desperate to ask again about Sam Thomas trying to grab Elaine, but couldn't bring herself to interrupt what was probably a form of catharsis.

'But once I'd heard about the cancer, it did make me feel better knowing she was going to die anyway. Does that sound horrible? She was murdered, but it wasn't as if the killer took away the next fifty glorious years. He didn't stop her getting off the streets and marrying someone rich and dying old, because those things were never on the cards. She was destined to die soon anyway because of that cancer. Die homeless on those streets. The killer just speeded things up a little.'

Elaine seemed to snap out of her trance. 'No, he didn't try to hurt me. It was a week or so after the funeral. He said he wanted to take my pain away. He grabbed my hand, but I pulled it away. I would have shut the door on him, but he looked horrified, as if he'd upset me. I think I felt a little sorry for him. I believed right then that he was also suffering because she was dead.'

The man in the garden turned and started to walk back

towards the house. Elaine said, 'Quick, go now, I don't want him to see you and ask questions. Go. My sister was killed by evil that's long gone and it's been too many years and you'll never solve it even if you really wanted to, so please, just go.'

Liz thought Elaine was a woman tormented by her own mind. Roiling in there was sorrow for a lost twin sister, but also derision because that sister had done bad things. She felt pity for her, but didn't like the woman and, certain there was nothing new to learn, was glad to get out of there. She left Elaine in the kitchen and went for the door.

But as she walked down the garden path, she heard Holly's sister's voice. 'It upset me that Holly wasn't one of the Yorkshire Ripper's victims.'

Liz turned to see Elaine standing in the open doorway, arms wrapped around herself as if cold.

'If my sister had been one of his victims, people would know her name, wouldn't they? She would be remembered. In a weird kind of way that I can't explain, I would feel that her murder wasn't for nothing, that it had meant something. That would take some of my pain away, even all these years later. Is that wrong?'

'You can't help what you feel,' Liz told her. It was all she could think of. And whether or not it soothed the grieving sister, she never learned: Elaine shut the door.

Back in her car, Liz found herself thinking about pain, and about Sam Thomas.

Earlier, she had read his original statement to the police, taken the day after Holly Ryan's murder. In that statement he had expressed a feeling that 'at least she no longer suffers the pain of cancer' and that he wished he could 'take her pain away'. In light of Holly's sister's claim that Sam Thomas had said something in the same vein to her and made a grab for her hand, these words uttered forty years ago niggled at Liz.

58

'I don't understand. I thought this was about my brother's murder.'

'It is,' Bennet told Darren. 'But we're also working a cold case. They're connected.'

'Connected?' Darren seemed to abruptly regain his composure. 'What do you mean?'

'Come on. A little further.'

'Talk to me, dammit.' He slammed a hand around Bennet's arm, but the detective carefully lifted it away. 'Everything will be clear in a few minutes.'

Bennet insisted that Darren crossed the bone-pipe first, carefully. On the other side, they continued walking. A short way ahead, just visible in the gloom, was another chain-link fence. Beyond was a row of houses.

'Now we're inside where the woodyard was. This was a driveway through it, to the rear, where there was an open space right where those houses are. All around here were work buildings and timber stacks and, over there, the main warehouse.'

Darren said nothing for a short time, until they reached the chain-link fence. 'I don't know why I'm here, detective. I think we should turn around.'

'Not yet, Darren. I paid ten pounds so you could park overnight. See those houses?'

Beyond the fence was a desolate street and on the far side of it a row of fenced back gardens and semi-detached houses. Bennet pointed. 'Just beyond those houses was a railway embankment. They got rid of that railway line. Just past the embankment, down the other side was Henney Road, where the Maximus nightclub was. Also gone. But I bet your memories of this place are very, very clear, aren't they?'

Darren didn't look at him. But nor did he look at the houses. 'I don't like what you're doing. I think it's time we went back. I think I should just fly home.'

Bennet pointed at one of the dark homes. Its back gate had an X of police tape strung across it. 'Let's go closer.'

Bennet grabbed the fence low down and tugged, and a flap opened like a door. Darren was shivering, and not from the cold. His arm needed another tug to get his legs moving. He had to duck to get through.

Still holding Darren's arm, Bennet led him across the road, towards the taped gate. The man went with his feet catching and scraping the tarmac, zombie-like, and saying nothing. The gate was unlocked. Bennet pulled the tape away and ushered Darren through.

As they entered, a man sitting and smoking on the back step jumped to his feet. Before he could speak, Bennet held up his warrant card and introduced himself. The uniformed scene guard tossed his cigarette.

'Unlock that door and take a five-minute break, officer,' Bennet told him. 'Go onto the street to smoke.'

The officer gave both men a long look, doubtless puzzled by what he was seeing. But he knew better than to question a higher rank. Within seconds three had become two. Bennet gave Darren a little nudge towards the back door. Here, he tightened his grip on Darren's arm. Still the man said nothing. Bennet pushed the door wide open to expose a dark kitchen.

'This is where you came with Holly Ryan. Looking for somewhere to have sex. That's how you got sex, Darren. Girls didn't like you. Because of your face, you had to pay for sex. You remember?'

This time Darren made a noise. It might have been just a croak. It might have been *yes*.

They stepped inside 88 Pond Street. Bennet flicked the ceiling light on, forcing both men to squint against the sudden glare. When Darren was able to focus, he saw Bennet pointing a finger. At the counter unit. At an empty space planned for a freezer.

'That's the spot, Darren. That's where your brother and Linda Squires had their mutilated corpses dumped. By a killer who knew that all three of you murdered a prostitute in that very same spot.'

59

———

Like a lot of ex-sports stars, Sam Thomas had found a way to continue doing what he loved long after age had ousted him from the top of his game. A sign at the gateway into Wheelbarrow Farm showed a picture of a cartoon off-road bike with a rider wearing an oversized helmet shaped like a falcon's head. The sign said LITTLE FALCONS MOTO ACADEMY. Judging by a list of 'Ride Times' Thomas had turned his farmland and his skills into a business.

She could hear the bikes before she could see them. Once she'd crested a hill, the farm was laid out a couple of hundred metres away. There was a long, one-storey brick building in an L-shape with smaller edifices dotted nearby. A fence had been erected in another L attached to the ends of the farmhouse to create a rectangle. The space within had been turned into a front lawn with garden furniture, like a regular garden out in a field. A hundred metres past the farmhouse was a tall wooden barn and between them were the bikes.

Thomas had thrown heavy earthmoving machines at the ground, to create the valleys and hills of a motocross track. Ten or eleven kids on small bikes were dipping and leaping in a clockwise circuit. Their parents lined a retaining fence, clapping or biting their nails or texting. A handful of staff inside the track stood around in trousers and T-shirts matching the colours of the academy's logo.

Liz drove along a fence-lined track and curved past the farm-house and towards a flattened dirt square passing for a car park. Just past were two gates, one to the right that ran away and cut through a high berm lined with trees about fifty metres away, and the other to the left, into the front garden. She parked here to use the gate on the left.

The building wasn't all brick. There was a segment near the end of the short crossbar that was wooden, like a block slotted in. Tools just outside and hanging on the inside of the open wooden door suggested it was a shed.

Sam Thomas was inside, working on his off-road motorbike. As she approached, she took off her wedding ring and slotted it away. He didn't see her until she was in the doorway and rapped on the wooden door. This close to the track, she could hear whooping children and parents yelling for less speed, above the engine noise.

Despite being in his sixties, the ex-rider for Sheffield Falcons was trim and handsome still, with a full head of grey hair spiked up like some Hollywood depiction of a veteran army colonel. She could also make out the bird tattoo on his neck, which was faded and a little blurry through age. A falcon, in honour of the speedway team he'd ridden for and the business he ran.

She held up her warrant card and introduced herself. 'A few minutes of your time, if you don't mind.'

'DCI?' he said, looking her up and down. 'Is it just you here?'

'Please put the spanner down and let's go into your house. And yes, it's just me here. Believe it or not, I'm a real, proper detective.'

He failed to catch the barb in her tone. 'This is about that murder over yonder, isn't it? I had officers here yesterday evening. They're going round all the farms. I told them I didn't know anything about it. How come they sent a DCI?'

'Well, this is about that investigation, but also about another. The murder of Holly Ryan back in 1979. Please put the spanner down.'

He dropped his tool. 'You're saying they're connected? Because it's the same area? For real?'

'Yes. And that's why I need to interview you. Can we go sit down somewhere?'

A grunt gave away his misery at the prospect. An impatient jerk of the head told her to follow him and be sharpish about it. Well, tea and biscuits were off the menu. He led her through the shed and a door in the wall that delivered them into what she could only describe as a bachelor's den. Here, with the pinball machine, games console and cinema screen, Sam Thomas had his bike memorabilia. Models, trophies and framed photographs were everywhere. The only seat was a beanbag. Thomas remained standing and she did the same.

'The police had quite an attitude with me all those years ago. I didn't enjoy their constant fascination with me. A few times since, when the case was reopened, or relooked at, or whatever, back they came with the same questions. And would you believe it, here you are back again. So let's make this quick, detective.'

Of the three people connected to the Holly Ryan case that she'd interviewed today, only a brain-addled prostitute hadn't treated her like something caught on their shoe. Her confidence was beginning to crumble. 'We've had new information. You might be able to help.'

He relented. A little. 'Okay. Sure. I will answer your questions, but do not ask me about my movements on the night Holly was killed. That's all in my various statements. Go from those, because nothing has changed, except it was a long time ago and today I could say something slightly different because of the passage of time, and I think you'd read that as suspicious. So ask me things that you might think will help you with your case. But don't try to seek an answer to Holly's killing by suspecting me.'

'I do need to ask you about your movements of two nights ago, if you don't mind. Just standard.'

He clearly minded. 'I was at home. Right here in this building. Same as I was way back when Holly was murdered. My mother was a witness back then, although one police officer told me this wasn't much of an alibi. My parents died years ago, and now I live alone, so feel free to tell me my alibi for these new killings is even flimsier.'

She knew Thomas's mother had made a statement that her son had been at home all night, practising in the dirt yard on his bike. Never a great alibi, family members. 'Thank you for your honesty. I had to ask. Back to Holly. You were fairly close to her and some of the other girls, right?'

'I felt sorry for them. I was a bit of a star in my day, and I went all around the country doing shows, and some were private exhibitions. I got to mingle with rich people, and famous people. Surround yourself with glossy, well-off women all day, it emphasises the downtrodden ones.'

'And in your statement from 1979, you say you never used these prostitutes.'

'I never did, not once. I was a star, I was young and handsome and had money. Remember what I said about the rich, glossy women?'

'So you were just a benefactor to these girls? You gave them money, and food, and condoms. I read that there was an event with a pair of men being aggressive. You intervened.'

'That wasn't Holly. But yes, two blokes thinking prostitutes love sex and would do it for free if the men were good-looking. I scared them off. But I wasn't a pimp, if that's what you're leaning towards. I took nothing from the girls. Nothing. I just felt sorry for them. For being forced into that lifestyle.'

'Tell me how you felt about the news of Holly's murder. How you found out. Did you continue to patrol the area afterwards?'

'I felt bad. I can't remember how I found out. Police, maybe. I stopped going back there.'

Lightning-fast answers. Thomas didn't like Liz's being here, even though she was trying to solve the murder of someone he knew and liked. 'She used to sleep in your barn, I understand. You let her.'

'I knew she was sleeping in the barn. Yeah, I let her. I mean, I never offered or gave permission, because she never asked. But I would sometimes see movement or hear something. The first time, I approached with my shotgun, thinking it was thieves. But then I saw her trying to tug down an old horse blanket from over the window, to use as a blanket. I never let her know I was there.'

'And why was that?'

Thomas seemed to have calmed a little. At least, he was answering her questions with a little less pace than originally. 'I felt I knew her quite well by then. But if she didn't have the heart to ask me, then I reckoned if she knew I knew, she might go elsewhere. At least here I knew she was safe.'

'You lived with your parents back then. Didn't they suspect anything?'

'By that time my parents had given up the hardcore farming lifestyle, so the barn was disused. The old root cellar had my father's radio transmitters in there, but he broadcast only on weekends. The rest of the time the barn was where I fixed up my bikes. I still use it for that these days. My parents barely went in.'

'And it was just Holly? None of the other girls came here?'

'There were a couple of occasions when I thought I might have heard a second voice, or just got the impression someone else was there. But I never approached after that first time. I think those other girls were brash enough that they'd tell me, or they would have asked to sleep there if they wanted to. But had places of their own. Holly was the only one who didn't have somewhere. That said, she never admitted it. But the other girls had told me she slept on the streets, or in that woodyard.'

Liz had to tread carefully here. Her detective's gut had spotted an error, but she didn't want to sound accusatory in case he shut down. 'I read your original statement to the police. I don't recall a mention of another voice heard in your barn.'

He looked puzzled, not angry at her question. 'I don't remember. That's not a big deal. I'm not saying she was with a punter. Just that sometimes I got the impression someone else was there.'

'Do you think it could have been her clients?'

'I'm not saying no, you understand? Just that I doubt it. Doubtful. Her working ground was that industrial estate over a mile away. No girl would travel so far with a punter, not on foot. I never saw or heard any vehicles. I only ever thought I heard Holly in the barn late at night, after the girls had stopped working.'

'So who do you think that second person could have been? Another girl after all? If it was after-hours.'

'I couldn't be certain of anything even back then, and so I haven't a clue today. Why is that a big deal?'

'An enemy? Could it have been a violent punter?'

'I don't have a clue. Not then, not now. Your train of thought puzzles me, because Holly wasn't killed in my bloody barn, was she?'

'Do you know anything about a pregnancy?'

He rocked back a step, as if her words had physical force. 'Holly? She was pregnant? I never heard that. Surely that would have been reported. That's a second murder.'

'I don't mean when she was killed, Mr Thomas. Years earlier. My information says she was kicked out of her home because she might have been pregnant. It was aborted.'

'Then I wouldn't know about a pregnancy, would I? I wasn't Holly's best friend. We didn't share dirty little secrets. I heard nothing about some old abortion, if there was one.'

'So you have no idea about a potential father?'

'That's the new angle, is it? An enraged dad out for revenge? Highly implausible.'

But was it? She remembered what DCI Bennet, who personified cool and calm, had said regarding his worries that his wife might secretly terminate their child: *I would have lost control... killed her.* 'I'm just acquiring information, that's all.'

He threw up his hands. 'Well I don't know about any abortion, or any angry father, or disgruntled punter. That case was a dead-end back then and forever will be. I don't care about the whys, detective. I'm not a God-fearing man in the least, but it's obvious poor old Holly was destined for a short life. It was the evil of man that opened her throat with a piece of sharp metal, but it was nothing human that put a giant cancerous tumour in her belly.' He looked skyward, raised his left hand and snapped it into a fist, as if snatching something out of the air. 'Holly, I wish I could help. If you were here with me, I would take your hand and soothe you.'

He put the fingers of his right hand against the back of his fisted left, and he raked them across the flesh, hard, fast, back and forth. 'I would take your pain away if I could. Only I can do it.'

As myriad red lines appeared on the back of Thomas's hand, Liz got to her feet, shocked. Her mind replayed the images of the destruction on the backs of the hands of the Pond Street victims. And then a similar injury, but far lighter, on Holly Ryan's.

Fingernails.

'Am I a damned suspect again? After all this time?' Sam Thomas yelled.

She barely heard, consumed by the image of an old crime-scene photo. The car-sized square water tank in the corner of the woodyard where Holly Ryan was butchered. Dense brush behind, so much better for hiding evidence. But ignored in place of the small space beneath the water tank. The picture was from about four metres away, and there was the fur coat underneath. Obvious. There was something wrong about the picture, but it continually hovered just out of her mind's reach. Until now.

'If I am a damn suspect again, this is a joke,' Thomas yelled. 'They took my fingerprints, they took my clothing, they searched my house and my barn. They came back years later and took my DNA. There was no match. Never was, never will be. It's a joke that you lot are back here again, asking me about this, suspecting me.'

Suddenly, that picture of the teddy coat stuffed under the water tank confused her no more. She felt a cold void open inside her. As Thomas took a step towards her, she blurted, 'I have to go,' and got quickly out of there.

60

'I had nothing to do with the murder.'

Darren Roddis had leaned against the kitchen wall, right across from the freezer space. Staring at it. For a long time he'd said nothing, and Bennet hadn't pressed. Just waited. In time, those words had spilled out. A sentence Bennet had heard many times, but this was different. This wasn't a man denying all involvement, he knew.

It was a tricky moment. Darren Roddis hadn't been arrested, so could be deemed to be 'helping the police with their enquiries'. But he hadn't been cautioned or offered a solicitor, either. Bennet's actions had gross misconduct written all over them. He had complained about Liz's bending of the rules, her inability to let go of a case that was no longer hers, and look at this. The correct thing to do was get Roddis to a police station, get him handed over to Liz's team, before things got pushed past the point of no return.

But here, now, Roddis was pliant, as planned. Bennet pushed: 'Not in a physical sense, maybe. But you were there.'

The perfect time to deny all knowledge of the murder of

Holly Ryan, right here where this kitchen now stood, forty years later. But Roddis remained mute. Bennet waited.

'My brother did it for me.'

'Carl and Linda hit it off. But you found it hard to attract girls. But Holly was a prostitute.'

Darren touched the dead, fake part of his face. 'It wasn't the idea from the start. But we knew the shortcut would take us onto that road where they worked. I'd told Carl that morning that I might try a prostitute if I was drunk. But I didn't honestly plan to. Not really.'

'Until you got here. And Holly was here. And then you did plan to. So you approached her.'

'No.' They locked eyes before Darren's returned to the freezer space. 'Carl did it. He flashed her some money. She took it. I didn't hear what was said. But she came over and started talking to me.'

'He paid her to have sex with you. In the woodyard.'

'No. No, it started with talking. We walked. We walked down the driveway, towards the back, where we were going to take a shortcut over the train tracks. Carl and Linda hung back. I walked with Holly and she talked about what she'd like to do to me. Sexual things. But I soon realised she thought Carl had paid her only to talk dirty to me.'

Bennet waited.

'When we got near the end, she tried to say goodbye. But that upset Carl. He wanted her to have sex with me. She said no, it was supposed to be just dirty talk. She said she couldn't have sex with me because she didn't sleep with men my age. But that was a lie. I knew it. I saw it in the way she couldn't look at me. Couldn't bear to see the ragged hole in my face. I knew she was disgusted by me. And Carl knew it. He was very protective of me.'

'They argued?'

'No. Just like that, he slapped her. She fell over, fell right out of her shoes. But she got up. She looked ready to fight. And she pulled out a knife.'

'Holly had a knife?'

Darren nodded. 'She tried to cut him, so he knocked her to the ground. Knocked her out. He was angry, but not because she'd threatened him. He was shouting at her because she'd turned me down. And he'd picked up a brick. Because she'd insulted me. I remember the Westminster chimes.'

Bennet knew what that was. It was the tune church bells played before they struck the hours. Roddis was referring to St Mary's and All Souls church, some three hundred metres away.

A pause. Bennet had to prompt him: 'Then what happened, Darren?'

'The bells rang. I didn't think he was going to do it, but the bell urged him, or made him react, or he used it to cover the sound. But he hit her. He brought it down. The brick. Onto her face. Each time. Each bell. He stopped when the bells stopped. I remember him standing there, with the brick raised, as if waiting for another ring of the bell. But it was over. And so was his... attack. He looked horrified, like he'd not been in control of himself, but had watched in shock of what his body had done.'

Roddis looked unsteady on his feet. Bennet told him to sit at the kitchen table, and Roddis just about collapsed onto a chair. Still he was mesmerised by that freezer space. It had been cleaned, but the man was likely imagining Holly's body there. Or his brother's and Linda's.

Bennet pulled out his phone and called a number. When it was answered, he spoke quietly, so Roddis couldn't hear. 'Hooper, did MIT 2 take the Pond Street CCTV from the neighbour's backyard yet?'

'We sent them a copy, yeah. We've still got the original disc though. No one's coming for that until tomorrow morning.'

'Get back to the office and get it. I think our man's on it, entering the house.'

'We've watched it over and over, boss. We see him leave, but not arrive. We watched it all the way back to the freezer delivery.'

'I know. Go back further.'

Hooper caught his breath. 'You know something, don't you? Are we going to solve this even though it's not our case anymore?'

'Go back to the night before. Start at... Think Norse worlds.'

He hung up, hoping his cryptic words didn't confuse Hooper. He squatted before Roddis, eye to eye, and told the man to look at him. 'You said your brother was horrified. Not that horrified, Darren. A crushed head wasn't Holly's only injury. She was further attacked, after her head was caved in, wasn't she?'

'We didn't know what to do. Carl thought he was going to go to prison. But Linda... she...'

'Linda Squires. She watched it happen. But it didn't bother her?'

'No. She was quite professional, I remember. She calmed Carl down. It was her idea to copy the murder.'

'An old murder from 1967. A docker called Harold Davies was murdered here, in this exact spot, when the timber yard was a school.'

Roddis nodded. 'There was that Yorkshire Ripper man around at that time, and we were scared that the police would think it was him. The whole of Yorkshire would investigate it, and we didn't want that. So it was Linda's idea to copy a murder she'd heard about. A boxer. There was a rumour he'd had a fight to the death for a thousand pounds. She said that the police would think the same man who killed him had done the woman. But it was many years before, so they'd look for an older man. We'd be too young to be considered suspects, even if the police found out we'd been in the area that night. We'd be safe.'

Bennet's father had heard the fight-to-the-death rumour, amongst others, but discounted it. 'There was another injury to that murdered boxer. His throat was cut. So you cut her throat, didn't you?'

That was a leading statement, but this wasn't a court. Bennet would worry about all of that later.

'Yes. But not me. Linda did it. Carl couldn't bring himself to. It was her idea, and so she picked up Carl's knife and…'

Carl's knife? He'd said it was Holly's. Might Darren be tilting this version of events in favour of his dead brother, and himself? Right now that didn't matter, because Bennet needed to hear the rest. 'What? What did she do?'

'She cut the woman's throat. All the way across.'

'And then what? There was more, Darren.' When Roddis didn't respond, perhaps not ready to add more, Bennet again led him. 'What else happened, while you were standing here in the woodyard? What happened to Holly's eyes in this place that had sawdust all over the ground?'

'Yes, sawdust. There was no sand like in the other murder. Linda did that, too. She took sawdust and put it in the woman's eyes.'

The confession was all there, wrapped and stamped and posted, but Bennet couldn't let the man stop while he was under momentum. 'And afterwards? What did you do? There was no attempt to hide the body.'

'No, we couldn't do that. That was too much. Linda threw the woman's shoes away over a fence, but after that we thought we'd been there too long, so we left. But Linda took the brick away and got rid of it somewhere. We just left as if nothing had happened and went to the party. Linda stayed away from us, so we could pretend we didn't know each other, and we just acted as if... like it had never happened. There were some knowing glances between us, you know, as people might if they have a secret, but we all kept our distance.'

'And after that night?'

'We got on with life. The police never got close to us. Carl and I never mentioned that night again. We put it behind us. And Linda, we never saw her again after that merger party. She didn't take her job at Carl's place. That was down to redundancy, maybe. Or she woke up the next morning and couldn't face us. You would think, being part of something like that, we would have kept in touch. I was surprised that Carl and her never became a couple. We'd shared something... momentous, a bond that you'd think would eventually draw us back together. But it didn't...'

Look at where we're standing, Bennet wanted to yell. *Think of Linda and your brother with their heads smashed in*. But he was reluctant to interrupt this confession, and said nothing.

'...the thing that upset me most of all was that I didn't have nightmares, didn't get depressed. As if we'd done nothing wrong. As if it was something minor. Does that make me a monster?'

Bennet didn't answer that. He was thinking of Liz's worries about Holly Ryan's coat, stuffed under a water tank. 'I need your information to be exact, Darren, if I'm going to help you get through this. I know it was a long time ago. But some of your details seem wrong. Holly's coat, for instance. It wasn't just the shoes you got rid of. You hid her coat under a water tank, didn't you?'

Darren Roddis shook his head. 'She was in a kind of tank top. She didn't have a coat.'

61

———

As Liz was driving to meet Bennet, her phone rang. It was one of her team from MIT 2, a pretty young DC tasked with whittling down the list of inmates of Leeds Prison at the time Carl Roddis was there. 'I found a good one,' the DC said. 'You were right about the long-term stalking.'

The focus had been on inmates released in the last few months, but Roddis's invisibility for the last three years had sparked an idea. What if his disappearance way back was connected? So Liz had moved the goalposts.

'I found someone who was convicted of murder in 1986.' The DC was almost breathless with glee. 'He was moved to Leeds Prison when he was twenty-one, and he was there when Carl Roddis did time. Get this...'

When the DC finished, Liz hung up and called Bennet, who answered with: 'Darren Roddis just confessed.' He recounted the man's story, but something about his dull tone told her he wasn't convinced of its accuracy.

She knew why. 'So if we believe his story, then he, the only living perpetrator, didn't harm Holly. He was only a bystander.'

'It also shifts a lot of the blame away from his brother and paints Linda Squires as the more vicious killer. It's very convenient. It could be true, he sounded sincere. But then he's had an eight-hour flight to rehearse it.'

'He's had forty years, Liam. Arrest him for me and I'll chip away at him at the station. Look, I found–'

'Liz, there's something else. Something a bit off, which I know you'll be interested in. He said Holly didn't have a coat.'

'I know,' Liz said, her mind spinning. She could hear someone crying down the line. Darren. 'Look, Liam, I can explain that later, but I found a name. Someone who was in prison at the same time as Carl Roddis, back in 2000. This man remained in prison until 2016. He was released the same month that Roddis disappeared. A man who broke the terms of his licence and vanished and hasn't been seen since.'

He made a satisfied sound.

'His name, Liam. His name is Dustin Falcon.'

Now he made another sound. 'Dustin Falcon. Why does that sound familiar?' Before she could answer, he had it: 'Sheffield Falcons.'

'But you won't believe the next bit–' she said, then stopped as she heard a scuffle, and a shout from Bennet, and a heavy thud.

And then the phone went dead.

62

When the world came back to Bennet, it was tilted. No, he was lying down. Liz was shaking him, imploring him to wake up. She was on her phone, calling something in. And he was lying on the floor, no clue how he got there, aware only of a terrible pain in his head. Until he heard her say the word *ambulance*, and then it all made sense. Darren, in a bid to escape, had hit him and fled.

She bent over him and thrust her balled-up coat against his head. It blocked his left eye, and he was blind. He wiped his right and it cleared. Blood. Now the world started to swim out of focus. But before it turned black, he saw, oh he saw, and he got his answer. There was Darren, not escaped at all, just sitting there. But not at the table this time. Now, he sat in the space for the freezer, just as his brother and their accomplice had been positioned.

Exactly as. Darren's face was gone, smashed into nothing, and his throat was cut. His head was tilted back, emphasising that throat gash. But that wasn't the reason. His head was tilted back so that his ruined eyes could be filled with sawdust.

63

––––––––

When the world came back again, it was tilted once more, and now vibrating. No, he was lying down again, and this time in a vehicle. Liz was by his side again, but not shaking him this time. He remembered that word, *ambulance*. He tried to sit up. It wouldn't happen.

She noticed he was awake and took his hand. 'The uniformed guard out back of Pond Street is headed to hospital, but he's okay. The one at the front knew nothing about anything until the ambulance arrived. And you'll be fine. Not handsome for a while, but you'll be fine. But stay lying down. Don't move.'

Something came back to him. He'd been attacked by Darren, who had esca... But then another piece fell into place. Not Darren. Darren hadn't attacked him. Darren was... dead. 'Falcon... we have to...'

He tried to sit again, but she put a lead weight on his chest and it nailed him to the bed. No, her hand. Just her hand. 'Stay down. It's being taken care of.'

'Where...'

'I called Jollops. He's leading an arrest team right now.'

She swam in and out of focus, like a ghost. 'You didn't go?'

'He offered. But I stayed with you to make sure you're okay. And I realised in all this time I didn't go to see Alan. He's out of hospital now. But I will tomorrow.'

Alan? He didn't know anyone called Alan.

'Falcon,' he repeated. Then his mind skipped back. 'Alan Bates. Your boss. My friend. I remember...' He tried to say more, but the world went away again.

64

───────

When armed officers from the Operational Support Unit came out of the path cutting through the high berm and into open land, they faced three targets. To the left was the farmhouse, ahead was the motocross track, to the right was the large barn. They split into three groups, to hit all targets in quick succession.

Unit one flicked on their gun barrel torches and bore down on the people on the motocross track, screaming for no one to move. A man and a woman were loading small bikes into a covered metal rack. They froze as what looked like invading aliens appeared out of nowhere in a blitz of light and noise.

At the same time, the farmhouse was invaded. These officers found Sam Thomas in his living room, reading with his feet up. When black-clad men burst in and screamed for him to get on the ground, he calmly threw his book aside and said, 'This better not be about Holly yet again.'

Meantime, the third, largest component of the strike team entered the barn. It was an open space, no alcoves or corners or upper floors or pillars to hide behind, thus easily secured within seconds of sweeping their torches around. Bike parts, tools and clumps of dirt from the field lay scattered around the wooden floor. The armed officers stepped aside for the detectives to enter. They crowded the doorway, aware that nobody was here. The hope was that their target was in the farmhouse, but soon the call came that Sam Thomas was alone in his home.

The detectives walked about, stepping carefully because not a square foot didn't have a bolt or a spanner or a discarded bent wheel spoke. They were hoping for a blatant clue that their target had been here, but it was DI Jollops who voiced the majority opinion: 'Miller's messed up. I'll dump her back into uniform for this.'

But then he noticed something peculiar. There was nothing uniform about the scattered detritus, except for one spot: a neat row of small xenon bulbs about two feet long, next to a box spilling them. They lay on a just-as-neat line of dirt. He bent down for a closer look and spotted a seam cutting through the dirt. It ran at right angles to the grain of the floorboards. He realised how that line of dirt and bulbs had been created.

Gravity. Sliding.

He got everyone's attention with a single whispered word: 'Trapdoor.'

65

———————

In kind of a mirror image of events back when he'd allowed Liz to question Lewis Carter at his station, Bennet had been asked if he wanted in on the interrogation of Dustin Falcon. The offer had come from his boss, Superintendent Hunter, who'd been contacted by Superintendent Allenberg, and Bennet didn't need detective skills to work out the next link in that chain. Despite being on medical leave, he leaped on the chance, much to his boss's surprise. 'Thought you hated all that fame and glory stuff?' Superhunter had said.

And he still did. But within the hour, he was parked outside Woodseats police station, watching the front doors. When he saw Liz emerge, he met her halfway.

'I got your message. Thank you,' he said.

'You played a major role. You deserve to see it to the end.'

She looked gorgeous, but also horrified by his bandaged face; she reached out to touch it, then seemed to change her mind and lowered her hand. Bennet prodded at the dressing himself. 'Doesn't hurt. Poke away.'

She lifted a finger and touched his face, but softly. She knew he had a fractured orbital bone and a deep, long laceration. The bandage covered most of one side of his head. He lifted a finger of his own, to touch her face. 'I see you have makeup on again. I've figured it out, finally.'

'Okay, Mr Psychologist, enlighten me.'

He said, 'When my son was a baby he had a milk allergy, kept throwing his bottle up, and he was in hospital for four days. A junior doctor looked after him. I remember wanting someone older, more experienced.'

She gave him a long look. 'I get the feeling this is about my makeup, of all things.'

'I was guilty of ageism, or whatever you want to call it. I think this is an attitude people have that worries you. I saw the way Hardy at the café in Wales looked at you. And the manager of the bingo club. Looks that said, how can this pretty young woman be a high-ranking detective? Aren't the best ones all grizzled old men with twenty years' experience? Some people have a retro idea that women detectives are there to make tea, do the paperwork, and hold the hands of abused women. And if one makes it to the elevated rank of inspector, well, she must have a father who's a chief constable... or she slept her way up the ladder.'

She continued to just look at him.

He carried on: 'I think this... let's call it the junior doctor image... is something that worries you. That youth and good looks mean you won't be taken seriously. So you intentionally go the other way and make yourself appear older and less attractive, more matronly, because you think it'll garner more respect.'

'And now? As you can see, I have makeup on. I epitomise the junior doctor image. Explain that.'

'You also wore it when you questioned our burglar friend, Lewis Carter. Because there was no need to present an image to him. He was a suspect. He wasn't someone you had to cosy up to. In fact, the way you smiled at him, I would say the junior doctor image was designed precisely to make him think you were innocent and inexperienced. No challenge to his intellect. Likely to make mistakes, be easy to fool. I think you question all suspects this way. I think it's why you appear young and pretty right now.'

Bennet reached into his pocket. She raised her eyebrows when he held aloft a wad of cotton buds. 'Are you joking?'

'I don't think you need an image of any kind. Not the matron, not the junior doctor. I saw you tie Lewis Carter in knots, and I saw you gain the respect of Charles Hardy, whether both wanted it or not. And the man we're about to question will stand no chance against you, either. You just about solved this one all by yourself. You're a brilliant detective. You just need to believe it.'

She gave a wry smile, but knew he saw right through it. 'We should go do–'

She'd turned to go, but he grabbed her arm. 'Liz, I know you want a famous murder case, but I also know it's not for a medal, or a promotion, and I know you don't want a bestselling biography or public adoration. You just want people to know you're good at your job.'

The praise seemed to embarrass her. 'We should go inside. You must be eager to start.'

Actually, no. He hadn't come here because he deserved to see the case to its end, or because he wanted to learn important answers. If this interview with Dustin Falcon hadn't involved Liz, he wouldn't have come.

Of course, he couldn't bring himself to admit as much to Liz, so he nodded, and in they went. Besides, he was still a detective and wildly curious because of it. When he asked what she'd learned in the twelve hours since Falcon had been arrested last night, she gave him a wink.

'In the interview, if you don't mind.'

He recalled those same words from her the other day. And his own response, which he now repeated: 'You want to keep it from me? You want me to learn your bombshell as you give it to the suspect?'

She continued the game with, 'You'll like it.'

He had no doubt.

66

Often the friends, family and neighbours of people outed as murderers professed confusion and disbelief. Not a reaction Dustin Falcon would ever generate. He had thick muscles, bad skin, bad teeth, a shaved head and surely a pound of jailhouse ink. A wedding photo of this fellow would look like a police mug shot.

He also had a wound on the back of his left hand.

Three police officers had escorted him everywhere once he'd been dumped at Churchfield Police Station in Barnsley, even to the toilet, but he'd been wordless and complacent throughout. No glazed eyes, so he wasn't in a state of disconnect that he'd soon rage out of. He seemed awake and aware. He was also someone who'd spent a long time adhering to prison regulations and hadn't put a foot wrong in years.

Back then, though, he'd made one error and there was light at the end of the tunnel. Recent behaviour had bricked up that tunnel for eternity. So they were still careful.

This caused issue when DI Miller entered the interview room with DCI Bennet and she told the police officers present to clear out. Falcon was cuffed, but in front and with his legs free.

Liz was a slim five-nine and Bennet was on crutches, vision impaired because of a bandage smothering the right side of his face.

But they had their orders. When the room was clear, both detectives sat before the monster on the other side of the table. Falcon stared between their heads, as if using peripheral vision to watch both at once.

Liz started the tape recording with a remote control. She introduced both detectives and Dustin Falcon and asked him to confirm that he didn't want a legal representative present. He shook his head. He rested his cuffed hands on the table. The back of his left hand was a mountain range of criss-crossed, raised ugly old scars. She informed the tape of his headshake.

After Bennet's arrival at the station, he and Liz had kept Falcon waiting another hour while they constructed an interview strategy. It was one they were happy with. Now, Liz slid her chair back a few feet as Bennet's shifted forward. She would play no role, for now.

Bennet started by asking Falcon about his ruined left hand. 'It looks like an old wound. How did you get it?' Bennet showed him a pair of photos. One male left hand, one female left hand. The back of each was torn up and crusted with dried blood. 'If your victims were still alive, their hands would heal and look like yours. Painful. It's all about pain, as we'll soon see. Tell me about these wounds.'

Dustin Falcon said nothing.

'We'll get back to the hands later.' Bennet showed him a series of photographs taken inside a small square space, nine feet across, with two rough walls of earth, one of stacked small fieldstones... and one of house bricks. It was the old root cellar under the Thomas barn.

Attached to the brick wall and hanging by string was a children's nightlight in the shape of a popular cartoon character, although the cellar had been brightly lit by police lights for the photography. In a corner was a sleeping bag on a pair of wooden pallets, near a cardboard box with a bin liner inside, filled with empty food tins and plastic water bottles. A water jug contained a brownish liquid later determined to be urine, but no container for faeces had been present. There were also stacks of tinned food and bottled water.

Three photographs got slid a little closer to Falcon. One was of a receipt from a home improvement retailer for a hooded plastic protective suit. Just the sort of thing that could help a killer, or forensic scientists analysing his handiwork, to avoid bloodying clothing or leaving fibres or hair or skin at a crime scene.

The next photograph was of a knife sticking out between two bricks in a wall; it had a worn, dirty handle, but a shiny, smooth blade. Bennet gave his opinion of what both items had been used for, but Dustin Falcon gave no reply.

It was the third photograph, of a large fieldstone in a corner of the cellar, that Bennet focused on. The stone was thinner in the middle, like a fat number eight, and there was a thick chain around it, secured by a padlock. The free end of the chain terminated in two leather restraints.

'We also found handcuffs in a small metal money box, along with syringes. We didn't find any stores of isopropyl alcohol, but we know this stuff, also called rubbing alcohol, is easily bought. You can get five litres for fifteen pounds. The syringes had traces remaining. Isopropyl alcohol can cause serious damage, even coma. You knew what you were doing while you kept Carl Roddis captive, chained to this fieldstone. The two of you, alone. You and the murderer of a prostitute called Holly Ryan way back in 1979. What did you talk about?'

Dustin Falcon said nothing.

'There's one thing you certainly talked about though. There

was another person, an accomplice who had helped to kill Holly Ryan. You wanted her too, you needed her, and Carl Roddis was supposed to tell you who she was and where she was. And that's where it went wrong. Because Carl didn't know where she was, and all he ever had was her first name, Linda, even though, back in '79, they knew they were going to be working together. I don't know how you found her. No strangers asked any questions at her house, or her workplace, or talked to any of her friends. Nobody saw her talking to any strangers. Would you care to fill in the blanks?'

Dustin Falcon said nothing.

'Maybe Carl had an epiphany one day. What we do know is that it took three years. For three years you lived like an insect, underground in that root cellar, perhaps venturing out only to follow clues here and there on Linda's trail. Carl didn't get to go out though. His autopsy showed severe malnutrition, muscle atrophy, pressure sores, and serious internal damage from the rubbing alcohol he ingested, numerous times daily, to keep him docile for day after day after day. He actually did, literally, vanish off the face of the earth.

'But then it came. That glorious day when you found Linda Squires, way down in Blackpool. I'm sure, soon, we'll have CCTV, or witnesses, that will put you and her together, making the journey back to Sheffield. Back to that grimy underground hole.

'After that you transferred them to the same place where Holly Ryan had been murdered, although that old woodyard is now a housing estate. But that wouldn't deter you. You got them into the house that stands where Holly was left dead. And there, in the same spot, you killed Carl Roddis and Linda Squires in the same method they used to kill their victim all those years before.'

After summarising this 'method', Bennet said, 'You didn't

break into the house though. You got in with a key hidden under a plant pot on the front porch. How did you know it was there?'

Dustin Falcon said nothing.

Bennet said, 'You have no family, no friends. You had all the time in the world to do this. You came across the waste ground to the rear, but entered through the front door and opened the back door, from inside. That's how you got your two victims into the kitchen. They were drugged on rubbing alcohol. They were like zombies, which allowed you to walk them across the waste ground behind the houses. Is there a vehicle somewhere? Dumped or destroyed after you used it to transport them to the house?'

Nothing from Falcon.

'Your research was good. Knowing the old woodyard was now a housing estate, that part was easy. To find that exact spot though. It took us a lot of poring over maps and pictures. I imagine that's how you did it. You were slightly off though. Workmen had to level off the ground before they built the housing estate. The actual spot would have been lower. In the basement, if there had been one. You floated the corpses about ten feet too high.'

Actually, Bennet wasn't certain about this. It was a guess based on a slight downward slope to the entrance to the woodyard. But he said it just to see Falcon's reaction. He was pleased to see disappointment upon the man's face.

'But you showed a keen desire to copy the murder from all those years before, and that made me wonder. What if it didn't just involve location and method? What if you also wanted to kill your victims at exactly the same *time* of the other murder.'

Nothing.

'And you knew what time because of the church bell that rang across the area. It struck nine times. Holly Ryan was murdered at nine o'clock. So, you would kill your victims at dead on nine o'clock, too.'

Bennet pointed a remote control at a screen on the wall. A paused video appeared. He explained for the tape – and for Falcon. 'We are showing Mr Falcon a recording from a backyard CCTV camera at number 86 Pond Street, next door to the crime scene. It shows the garden of number 88. The time is 10.16pm on Sunday the 8th of December. That is the day *before* the murders.'

He set the video playing. Next door to May's, a figure was seen morphing out of the deep blackness beyond the road at the end of the gardens, and then it crossed that road. But not one figure. Two. One seemed slumped, held up by the other. They got over the wall, and through the gate, and came up the path. Despite the quality being so bad that determining identity was impossible, it was clear one figure was assisting the other. Both vanished below the screen, which meant they'd entered the house. A minute later, one figure made the return journey and vanished into the deep space.

But it came back. Twelve minutes later.

As before, it was accompanied by a second figure. The event repeated. When the figures vanished out of the bottom of the screen again, Bennet stopped the video.

'You had missed your deadline, Mr Falcon, isn't that right? You arrived at the house with your victims over an hour too late. But you were desperate to get this thing right. So, you waited. You spent the whole day in the house with your victims, waiting for the next evening. Somehow, you hid these two still-alive people when a man turned up to deliver a freezer. He didn't realise a thing. He put the freezer in place, which you then had to move. And still you waited. And at the right time, at the stroke of nine o'clock in the evening, you replayed a forty-year-old piece of history. In the same spot, at the same time, by the same method, you killed Carl Roddis and Linda Squires.'

Falcon didn't respond.

'You left out the back, across the waste ground. But you didn't leave straight away. Not until 3.22 the next morning. Did you sit and watch the bodies? Did that give you a thrill?'

Nothing.

'But you weren't finished. The bloodlust wanted more. There was a third person you wanted, the one who had watched the other two slaughter that woman all those years ago. But you had no idea where he was, or maybe you knew he was in America but that was still a world away and out of reach. You couldn't possibly kidnap him and get him across the ocean and all the way to that house. But you didn't need to. You knew he would come here, once he learned of his brother's murder. He would come to talk to the detectives. He would want to see the crime scene. All you had to do was wait and watch. And he would walk right into your hands.'

Dustin Falcon said nothing.

'And then you killed him, and you nearly killed me, you bastard,' Bennet yelled. 'Do you deny any of this?'

Dustin Falcon said nothing.

Bennet felt a rawness in his throat from the shout and his hands shook. Liz was watching him in wonder and he knew his outburst had stunned her, if not Falcon. If this was anger, he didn't like it.

Under the table, Liz touched his hand reassuringly, and the whitewater adrenaline in his veins slowed to a trickle. 'That covers the *how*. Now, Mr Falcon, it's time for the *why*.'

Then Bennet pulled his chair back two feet, to show he was removing himself from the spotlight. And Liz pulled hers forward.

67

———

Like Bennet, Liz started by asking Falcon about his ruined left hand. 'It looks like an old wound. I know how you got it.'

Dustin Falcon just stared between them. No question had been asked.

She moved on. 'August 15th, 1986. You were arrested and later convicted for murder. You beat to death a fourteen-year-old boy. While he slept. You claimed he was bullying other boys and you sought vengeance for them. For that crime you went to various youth custody centres and, at twenty-one, were transferred to Leeds Prison. You were there until 2004, when you were transferred to another prison. You were eventually released on licence in June 2016. There's two dates that are important here.

'One is your 2004 transfer. It's what I would call a hoodoo. One of many. But we'll get to that a little later. The other important date is the year 2000. That was when Leeds Prison got another inmate. A man called Carl Roddis.'

Dustin Falcon just stared between them. No question had been asked.

'Carl Roddis wasn't a convicted murderer, like you. As far as anyone knew, he was just a guy being punished for beating up his wife's brother. He might have felt vulnerable. To up his status, get some respect, he boasted to his fellow prisoners about a previous crime. There's a real behaviour spectrum in prison, because one day you'll tell how you stole a chocolate bar and someone will snitch to get a reduced sentence. But generally, it's a case of *what happens on tour, stays on tour*. Carl Roddis got lucky because his boast stayed on tour. Nobody outside those walls heard his claim that he'd murdered a prostitute called Holly Ryan twenty-one years earlier. Inside those walls, perhaps prison life became a little easier for him, and a few months later he was gone and forgotten. And his story, by far not the most outrageous a prisoner has ever told, was soon forgotten too. But not by you.'

Dustin Falcon just stared between them. No question had been asked.

'It must have burned. There you were, continuing to serve time, many long years still ahead of you, and the killer of Holly Ryan had walked free. It continued to burn inside you for the next seventeen years, until your release on licence in June of 2016. There you were, out in the world, and there Carl Roddis was, out in the world. Within a week of your release, you broke the terms of your licence and disappeared. The same month, Carl Roddis also seemed to vanish off the face of the earth.'

Dustin Falcon just stared between them. No question had been asked.

'And the reason for it all? For that, we need to go back. In 1982, as a child, you were arrested for stealing bread. You refused to talk about your parents and didn't give the authorities a residence or any family names. The police put your face in local newspapers, hoping someone would recognise you. They looked at hospital records, and they looked into birth announcements in papers from the year they suspected you were born. But they found nothing. DNA as a means of matching people wasn't around until a few years later.

'So, with no answers, they put you into care. Back before 1983, unregistered people born in the UK were automatically issued British citizenship. So it was a quick process compared to today to get you a name you liked and make you a child of the state. Because of your lack of birth record and being brought up on the streets, you were nicknamed Tarzan and Lord Greystoke, while others called you Grey Blood. But the name you picked was Dustin Falcon. We'll get to why that was soon.'

Dustin Falcon just stared between them. No question had been asked.

'A few years later, DNA was the new thing and we had the ability to test for your maternal or paternal heritage. But the story of the unknown boy had been forgotten. By now he had a new name and was lost in the prison system, doing life for murdering a bullying boy in a care home. So nobody thought to do that test. Nobody cared. Here's where we return to the year 2004, and the hoodoo. It's a term I use. Of all the luck. Like Sod's Law. A fluke event at just the right time to make things awkward. For us, not you.

'A few years earlier, the government had begun the DNA Expansion Programme, designed to get all convicted criminals onto the DNA database. That programme could have finally given us some answers about you, but your transfer out of Leeds Prison in 2004 happened a month before that facility was due its DNA sampling run. Even worse, the prison you were sent to had already had a DNA run amongst its prisoners just five months earlier. Like so many still incarcerated, you slipped through the net. Still no answers about you.

'We have your DNA now, though, and soon we'll have proof of what I already know. In the last few hours, we just got word back from our lab that we have a profile from DNA found on a brick fragment at the crime scene. I think you know it's going to match yours. But do you know why these answers have dodged us for so long?'

Dustin Falcon turned his stare upon her. A question had been asked. But he said nothing.

'Damn hoodoos, Dustin. Holly Ryan's autopsy discovered a giant tumour in her uterus, which had enlarged it. The damage from that tumour disguised the fact that her uterus was already extended. From giving birth.'

68

———

'Holly's sister, Elaine, thought Holly might have given birth, so she searched birth and death records. But she found nothing. Holly feared her child would be taken away into care, because she was a homeless prostitute. So, sometime around October 1971, Holly gave birth to the baby alone, perhaps down a dark alley behind a bin somewhere. The baby was unregistered, invisible, and for almost eight years he was by her side on the streets. Until her death forced him to go it alone. Nobody notices an adult on the streets, but a child is different. Somehow, though, he remained hidden and alone on the streets, for roughly two years. And then he was arrested for stealing bread.'

Upon arrest today, Dustin Falcon had said nothing. He'd accompanied the police to the station without argument, and performed the routine of a mouth swab, photographs and fingerprinting without a single word uttered. This continued silence during interview hinted at an unbreakable policy. So it was a hefty surprise when, without a question asked, he spoke.

'Elaine.' He sounded like someone trying a foreign term. His voice was a little high for someone so big and rugged. He said the name two more times. Then: 'I didn't know. I mean, I knew. There's always family, in the biological sense.'

'She tried to find you, Dustin. She wanted you to exist, to be real. After your mother's murder in '79, she searched care homes. But you didn't get arrested for stealing bread and thrown into the care system until '82. You missed each other by a narrow window of time. We'll tell her about you, rest assured. Would you like to meet her?'

'No.'

'If it's because she waited until after the murder to search for you, I think I can explain that. She wanted–'

'A reminder? A piece of her sister back? A legacy? It does not matter. They abandoned my mother. This auntie, this Elaine, she is family only biologically. That applies to whoever else out there survives still. Tell them about me, that is your duty, but there will be no meeting. The next time I enter a room like this, with its one-way mirror, I will hide my face. Just in case you bring them in to watch me from next door like a zoo animal. Don't bring those people up again, please.'

She had done her duty by informing the man before her of his remaining family, but he was a quadruple murderer and she wasn't here to hold his hand. She moved on.

'But you didn't just live on the streets with your mother. Perhaps that was her way before you arrived, but after that she needed a warm, safe place for her baby every night. She knew a place. A place that you soon came to associate with safety, because it was warm and quiet and while you were there, your mother wasn't working, she was by your side. And you were drawn back there years later, as a grown man released from prison. For three years, with a prisoner, you lived in that root cellar under the barn on Wheelbarrow Farm.'

'Correct.' No denial, but nothing further. Liz continued.

'The owner was a man called Sam Thomas. He told me he

sometimes thought Holly had a guest in there. But it wasn't clients. It was little baby you. She took you there because she knew that Sam Thomas was a nice man. He couldn't ever be told about you, though, in case he told the authorities and you were taken away. But you knew about him. I think that your mother talked to you about him. The only nice man you ever heard about. He wanted to take your mother's pain away after she died. If only he could have taken that pain out of her and put it into himself. He even tried to help your mother's sister, Elaine, by trying to take her pain, too.'

She looked down at the back of Falcon's ruined left hand. 'You would have wanted to take your mother's pain away. I think she showed you how to do this, which Sam Thomas had showed her.'

He turned his hand over to display the palm and hide his wound.

'So Sam Thomas was a good man in your opinion. Perhaps the only good man in the world. Later, when the authorities put you in care and offered you a new name, you remembered this man your mother talked about, who had a falcon tattoo on his neck and who rode for the Sheffield Falcons.'

'That is why, yes. Well done. Can we hurry along, please?'

If he was eager to know how much she knew, she was happy to oblige.

'But your mother had to keep working. She would keep you nearby when she worked the streets, wouldn't she? Money had to be made, for food. And it was the only way she knew how. But it wouldn't do to cart a little boy around the city at night. He couldn't be kept safe in the major red-light areas, with all that danger. She needed somewhere safe, like a site closed at night. Quiet. Safe. Like Harrison's Timber Merchant, which was right in the middle of a known prostitute area. Perfect.'

'Very good. Next?'

'Plenty of places in that woodyard to keep you safe and dry while she worked. Like the water tank. There was no room for an adult to slip underneath it, but a child of almost eight years of age could. It was where you slept, wasn't it? With your mother's fur coat as a pillow. When we get a profile from your DNA, it will match the unknown one found on Holly's coat, won't it?'

'Next?' he pushed.

'And that's where you were when she was murdered, isn't it?'

Dustin Falcon gave no pause or attempt to deflect or deny, and he wasn't floored by how much the police knew.

'At last, we get to your point. How did I know how and precisely when my mother was butchered? And now you have that answer.'

Falcon turned to Bennet. 'You wanted some blanks filling in? I watched that house for months. When I was ready, when I had finally found the woman, if the owners had been at home, I would have tied them up, out of the way. But they went on holiday. That's what you might call a reverse hoodoo. I knew about the front door key under the plant pot. I also knew the location of all the cameras on the street and the front of the house was barely covered. Once I was inside, I climbed out the front window to lock the door. I put that key back, because I knew I was going to be there all day. It would raise suspicion if someone who knew about that key paid a visit and it was missing. The delivery driver, for instance. When my job was done, I again exited through the window to fetch that key. I'm not even sure why.'

Falcon stroked the sea of terrible scars on the back of his hand. 'And now you both have all the answers you will ever need. I will plead guilty, by the way. No fight. So we don't need this show. I know solitude, I know abuse, I know captivity. You should fast-track my conviction. I should go back to my cage. Better for all if I just become lost again. So, are we done here?'

Liz pulled her chair closer to the desk, to promote the fact that she wasn't ready to end this interview yet.

'You sound eager to spend the rest of your life in that cage you mention. Are there no regrets?'

'Do you know why I took the front door key? Why I locked up the house? I didn't want anyone finding the bodies that night. I didn't care if they were found the next morning, which they were, or if they rotted there for two weeks. But I needed my mother's killers to sit there alone, dead, for one whole night. Because that was what happened to my mother. Alone. Dead. All night. I got revenge for her, and that was all that mattered to me. My soul is clean. My only regret, by the way, is that the woodyard was gone. I would have liked every building, every piece of wood and tuft of grass to have been exactly as they were back then. That is all. You know how and you know why. Now return me to my cage.'

'We do know why. But it wasn't revenge. I don't think your soul is cleansed at all.' She reached out and snatched Falcon's ruined hand. 'This is why.'

He didn't fight her grip, even when she raised his hand, the ruined flesh a focal point between them.

'Your mother's killing haunted you for all those years. You were constantly in pain, and your mother wasn't around to take it away from you. But her killers could, couldn't they? The scientists who examined the wounds on the backs of your victims' hands believe a weapon was used, because the injuries are so severe. But I don't believe that. I believe your rage and sorrow were so severe that you fought with all your strength to force them to take your pain, with your bare fingernails. They gave you that pain, and it was their obligation to take it back. You relive that horrible event every moment of every day, and now I want you to relive it for me, Dustin. Here, in this room, out loud. Relive it.'

Dustin Falcon stared at her – through her – for a few seconds, no emotion, his eyes no window inside his head. Then he closed those eyes, slowly. She knew he was cycling back. Back along an oft-treaded corridor in his mind, rewinding the years, to find a door into the hell of that long-ago night.

69

———

I *kicked the bucket, Mummy.*

That usually means something else, Dustin, Mummy says. She rubs his bare left foot. *When you got up to pee?*

Dustin nods. *It didn't spill, though, and I emptied it. What does kick the bucket mean?*

It's a saying. She scratches at the back of her hand. *It means to die.*

I don't want to die. I don't want you to die.

None of us is dying for a long time yet, Dustin. Give me your hand. Now, you see what I'm doing?

Why are you scratching your hand?

My friend showed me this. You remember, him with the motorbike?

Falcon Man?

Yes. When I hold your hand and I scratch my own flesh, I am taking away your pain. Can you feel it leaving your body? I am transferring it from you to me. The greater my pain becomes, the less yours is.

I don't want you to feel pain, either.

But it's better this way. Better me than you. I don't want you to suffer. Now, you know I have to go to work in a minute, don't you? And you're going to sleep.

Will you stay near again?

Always, Dustin. I'll be right here in this woodyard, as always. But you won't see me. But I'll see you. As always. I promise. So now you promise.

I promised last time. I said I'll never leave while you're working. Why do I have to promise every night?

Because I like to hear it. And then, afterwards, we'll go buy some food. Now give me a kiss.

She stands up and he copies. They exit from between the tall stacks of wood and, hand in hand, dash across the open part of the woodyard, towards the water tank. She removes her teddy coat, rolls it into a ball and pushes it under the metal box, as far as she can reach. Then she pulls her son into a hug. She kisses his head through his grey woolly hat. He squeezes back hard.

Won't you be cold, Mummy?

Don't worry about me. Go under now.

He gazes up at her. She reaches into her mouth and removes a hair. Dustin spots a hairy bit from his hat in her hair too, and he plucks that one away. Then he gets onto his belly and drags himself under the water tank. He likes the darkness beneath the tank, and it's warm here despite the cold metal of the tank pressing upon his arm and hip when he lays on his side. But he hates that his mother cannot fit under with him and sleeps alongside it.

Sometimes, when he's lonely, he shifts to the edge, to be close to her, to give her some of his warmth, and he decides he will do that tonight when she returns. When he's laying with his head on his mother's comfy coat, he can see her squatting and bending sideways so she can look at him.

Don't come out, even if you hear me. Even if I'm shouting. If I sound hurt.

I will hurt anyone who hurts you, Mummy. I promise.

There's no need. It will all be fine. But don't you come out at all, not all night, do you understand? And I'll be back soon. And then we'll go to our special place to sleep and in the morning we'll go to Wimpy.

And buy me a bird picture like Falcon Man's.

She laughs. *I told you, my friend has that tattoo because it means something. It's the team he rides his bike for. You only get a tattoo when it means something. Because something is important to you. Maybe in ten years you can have one. Now go build a log house. I'll be back, I promise.*

It's a tactic for getting him to sleep. Instead of counting sheep, he is to imagine himself hauling wood from around the yard to construct a house. It usually works and does this time, because the next thing he knows, he jerks awake at a shout. A male voice.

Kiss him, you bitch.

As he lies there, with the ground below and the metal of the water tank just inches above, he sees someone run into the open ground. In the moonlight, he can see it's his mother. He is about to shout for her when another figure appears. Behind her. Chasing. A man.

Shocked, he watches as the man catches up to his mother, right in the centre of the open ground, and grabs her hair to haul her to a stop. *Kiss him*, the man shouts again.

And now two more people arrive. Another man, with a funny face, and a woman. The first man holds Dustin's mother, pointing at the other man. *Kiss him. A dirty whore doesn't care about his face. Kiss him.*

Mother shakes her head. Dustin wants to call out, but he remembers his promise. He always keeps his promises.

And then the man hits her. Hard. She falls onto her back and her shoes come loose, right off her feet. He picks up a brick. And then Dustin hears the loud chime of the church bell, usually such a sweet sound, but terrible and frightening tonight.

What happens next is impossible to watch, and he screws his eyes shut. He tries to imagine himself with more wood, carrying stacks of it, but the sound of his mother, screaming, shreds this image, and he cannot sleep. His eyes open. And he watches.

His fingers scrabble in the dirt and land upon a sharp stone. He digs it into the back of his left hand and draws it this way and that. He can feel blood. His mother is making terrible noises and he scrapes at the back of his hand even harder.

The pain is horrendous and tears cascade down his face. But that pain is good, because he is drawing it away from his mother. And soon it begins to work because her screams become moans, her flailing arms and legs begin to slow down. And then those moans falter, fade, die. But the man hits her again, and again, as the church bell fills the air like thunder.

Soon, there is no sound at all. The three adults have not finished with her though. The man with the brick pulls out a knife, but the woman takes it off him. They do something to his mother's neck. They do something to her eyes. One throws away her lovely red shoes.

And then they leave.

His mother is still out there, thirty paces away, lying on the ground. She is not moving. Her head looks to be a funny shape, hair seems wet, but he cannot see her face because it is turned away. One arm is bent under her back in what looks like an awkward position.

He wants to go to her, but again remembers his promise. So he shuts his eyes. Inside his head, he lifts planks of wood and stands them up. They will become the walls of the log house.

Despite the pain, he sleeps. He knows this because when he wakes, it is daylight. He can hear a metal scraping sound that he knows is men sliding a metal sheet across the river, to create a bridge into the woodyard. That noise is his mother's alarm, because, on those days when they don't sneak into her friend's barn to sleep, it is the cue to leave. Men are coming to work in the woodyard and they cannot stay here. His mother always wakes at that scraping noise, gets him up, and then they leave.

He scrambles out from under the water tank. But his mother doesn't get up. She has not heard the noise. She is in the same position as before, with her head turned away, hair matted with something sticky, and that arm still bent under her. She has not moved all night, he knows.

Now he can hear voices. Men, coming this way. *Mum*, he calls, *we can't stay.*

She doesn't move. But he does. It is what she would want. Clutching his blood-encrusted hand inside his coat, he flees for the fence, and over, and up the hill towards the train tracks. He stops dead, realising he has left Mummy's coat behind.

He hears a shout of *Jesus Christ, here, quick* and ducks behind a bush, thinking he's been spotted. But when he peeks through, he sees a man standing by his mother, staring at her. Other men rush to his side. Only then, with the panicked way they are shouting, does he finally accept that his mother is hurt and will not be following him. But she will come later. She has never broken a promise to come back to him.

He knows what to do. He will go to the barn because Mother told him many times, *If ever we get split up and I cannot come back to you, go to my friend's barn. Hide there and I will come to you. I promise.* And she will do that, he knows, because she has never broken a promise. So she will come to him tonight. And he will wait. And if not tonight, then she will come tomorrow. But he will wait, because he also made a promise.

And he doesn't break his, either.

70

TWO DAYS LATER

The house was a modern affair just outside Sheffield, in a village called Low Ending. It was listed as a cottage but looked to Bennet like an end-terrace. If there was a cottage-like aspect, it was the ivy clinging to every inch of the pinkish walls. There was a sleek Jaguar XJ in the driveway.

Bennet's passenger accompanied him to the door, along with two uniformed officers. The woman who answered, who he already knew as Carla Murray from a phone call to her arranging this appointment, was early thirties, pretty, with big eyes and sharp cheeks and short blonde curls more fitting to a toddler. She wore a trouser suit, having returned from her city job for this meeting, and oozed elegance.

She also wore a smile, which worried him. When he'd called her about her grandfather, to have her present when the police spoke to him, she had asked Bennet if this was about that 'shed thing'. No, he'd said. It wasn't about Jack's broken-into shed the other week. A more serious matter.

That should have alerted her to the fact that, well, this was a more serious matter involving her grandfather. The two uniformed cops standing behind him should have conveyed that message too. Nope. Not with that smile.

He introduced himself and his 'civilian observer' and was invited in. Her father had just had lunch, she told them, but she'd missed hers to meet the police here. Could they do this quickly? She had important things to do. A hint of impatience there, but still that smile.

The living room was bland and old, with a few touches that appeared to be a woman's, like the plethora of vases of flowers. Jack Murray himself was old and bland too, again with a woman's input, like his GRUMPY OLD GIT T-shirt. He sat in a wheelchair between two armchairs, six feet from a TV that was at least twenty years younger than the next newest item here, flowers aside.

He turned his head to gawp at his new guests. But without any sort of realisation or recognition. Then he stared at the TV again. One of those shows in which members of the public refused to part with sentimental jewellery passed down from an ancestor, until an antiques dealer waved cash under their noses.

He was eighty-three but looked a hundred. Pale, thin and wrinkled everywhere, as if overnight he'd shrunk from ten feet tall. Bennet also knew, from the distant eyes, that today was going to be a problem.

Which the granddaughter confirmed when she said, 'He won't understand why you're here, what you want from him. I can get through to him. So talk to me.'

The same thing she'd said on the phone. Bennet had assumed it was a defence tactic to make sure nobody took advantage of her granddad. Or maybe a nosey tactic, to make sure she got some good gossip. Now he knew it was neither. It was no more or less than she'd said.

'It's a delicate matter,' Bennet said, buying time while he thought about how best to do this.

'I understand that,' Carla said, eyeing the officers behind him. 'Look at my grandfather. He's old and frail and he won't remember what he hears today come tomorrow, or even later today. Don't worry about what you say. Say it to me, and say it straight. This isn't about the shed break-in, is it?'

They were all stood in the centre of the living room, which he didn't like. But he wasn't sure he wanted to sit either.

'No. I said it wasn't, Ms Murray. Your grandfather was arrested in 1988, wasn't he?'

Her shoulders slumped. 'Oh please. Tell me this isn't about an assault over thirty years ago?'

Her scorn gave him resolve. He no longer felt like an intruder. The nerves started to slip away. 'He put a ten-year-old in hospital. Cracked him over the head with his cane.'

'He was protecting an eight-year-old. Me. We'd gone for a walk in the park. Four thugs who'd just learned about girls decided they wanted to see one naked for real and were not about to take no for an answer.'

'I don't doubt his intentions. I'm a father myself. I would have done the same thing. But laws are laws and he was arrested, and his DNA was taken. We're here because that DNA has been matched to... another crime.'

'Another crime? Crime? Protecting his granddaughter is a crime suddenly?'

She'd missed the point. But, as he watched, her face changed as that point prodded her like a spear.

'Look at him. What crime? Do the maths, you silly fool. He's eighty-three years old. He can't walk, hasn't been able to for years. When was this supposed crime my infirm grandfather apparently committed?'

'I did the maths, Ms Murray. That's why I know your grandfather was thirty-one years old when this crime occurred, and I'm sure he could walk just fine back then.'

He was appalled to find that her expression of repulsion made him think of a sex doll with its eager mouth. '1967? Are you for real?'

Quick with the maths. A City banker, perhaps? 'There's no statute of limitations on murder.'

Bennet noticed that the old man, who looked as far from a killer as you could get, had been glancing their way throughout. Not like someone keeping tabs though. Much as you might turn your head towards flickering movement.

Now, as his granddaughter collapsed on the sofa and burst into tears, the old man watched all three of them with confused interest, as if he sensed they were talking about him. Like a toddler who grasps the admonishing tone but not yet the words his parents are using. Even the sight of his distraught granddaughter barely evoked a change in emotion. Bennet found that his imagination couldn't conjure a picture of this man in court for a murder trial without him wearing that GRUMPY OLD GIT T-shirt.

We're cops, here to do a job, he told himself to keep the resolve intact. 'He lived in Sheffield in 1967, didn't he?'

She looked at him through her tears.

'He was questioned about a murder in 1967, wasn't he?'

That stopped the tears. As if she had begun to accept the truth. Or at least the possibility.

She stuttered through: 'Yes. I know. Someone from his boxing club was killed. The police questioned them all. There was no proof...'

'Now there's proof.' He explained. In 1967 a dock worker

called Harold Davies was murdered. The police recently got Davies' DNA off an old boxing trophy on display at a gym where he used to train. It matched DNA on the murder weapon – he didn't mention Charles Hardy, the former policeman who'd stolen that murder weapon from the crime scene. 'There was another DNA profile on that murder weapon, which we matched to your grandfather.'

'This is preposterous,' she said, standing again. He saw that toughness he'd guessed at earlier. 'You want to just arrest him? Take him out? He's never out of that chair, or this house, and you want to just take him away? He won't understand. He needs constant physical care. Are you going to wipe him after the toilet? He's upset by new surroundings. You're not just taking him out of here to put in a prison for a day or a year or however long he lives. He tried to kill himself when my grandmother died and I'm all he's got. I'm calling my boyfriend. He's a solicitor. You just keep your hands off him. I'm calling.'

'Hello,' the old man croaked, and raised a hand for a sort of wave. Some sort of neurological delay there, maybe: perhaps responding to their arrival five minutes earlier. Lord knew when this poor sod would finally understand what was happening here.

Carla went into the kitchen for her mobile phone, presumably. Bennet relaxed. He wanted the boyfriend solicitor here, to ease his own burden. The old man was no flight risk, and the courts wouldn't mind another hour tagged onto the years they'd waited, so Bennet called out, 'We'll wait in the car. Please don't try to take your grandfather out of the house.'

But when he turned to go, the old man said, 'Inspector Bennet.'

Shocked, Bennet turned back to him. But the old man was looking past him, at the civilian observer, who had remained silent so far. Bennet took a step back so he could watch both men. Both in their eighties, yet they glared at each other like gladiators about to duel.

'You know why we're here,' former Inspector Ray Bennet said.

The old man gave a slow nod. 'I think so. I forget my granddaughter's name sometimes. But I'll always remember Harold Davies.'

'And that night? You remember that night?'

Another slow nod. 'Actually, no. Shapes in my mind. Half-pictures, I guess. But that doesn't matter, because it's upstairs. Three, three, four, four.'

'What's upstairs?' Bennet said. 'What is that, a code?'

'I remember a lass. Yes, there was a lass. It was about her. He cheated. I think.'

'Cheated at what?' Ray said. He knelt before the man, faces level. Bennet glanced towards the kitchen, praying the granddaughter wouldn't come in during this pivotal moment.

'I got the lass in the end,' the old man said.

'You're going to lose her,' Ray added.

The old man hung his head. 'I lost her four years ago. No problem remembering that. I'm a burden to this one.' He jabbed a thumb towards the kitchen. 'I can make amends finally. The guilt for Davies is long gone. But you came here. That crime bothers you. I don't know you though.'

'I was a detective investigating that case. It was the only murder I failed to solve.'

The old man looked at Bennet. 'Quick. Upstairs. Three, three, four, four.'

'And what are we going to find upstairs?' Ray said.

'That you didn't fail. I think.'

Bennet headed for the door and took thickly-carpeted stairs to the first floor. On the top landing, the door dead ahead was wide open, revealing a bedroom with an orthopaedic bed and a

Zimmer frame beside it. He stepped inside. The room stank. The first thing he saw were framed photos of a woman at various ages. The most recent suggested she was about sixty. He figured this was the dead wife, gone now at least twenty years.

Then he saw the safe. It was a small thing, more like a toy than a security product, sitting on a shelf above the bedside table and screwed to a wall bracket. And it was dial-combination.

Heart pounding, Bennet crossed the room and input the code with shaking fingers. The door popped open. Inside was a small Tupperware box of jewellery and a folded plastic document wallet of paperwork, but that was all. Bennet reached for the wallet, and that was when he saw something heavily Sellotaped to the inside left wall. A folded piece of paper. There was nothing written on the taped side. He peeled it away.

The paper was old and yellowed and brittle and he was careful when opening it up. It was a handwritten letter. As he read, he realised that he was holding something that Jack Murray must have composed not long after his wife died.

And that Jack Murray hadn't tried to commit suicide because of her death. A death, but not hers. And he'd kept this letter hidden ever since.

I AM THE MAN WHO KILLED HAROLD DAVIES. I AM WRITING THIS BECAUSE I HAVE DECIDED TO TAKE MY OWN LIFE TO JOIN MY JOANNE IN HEAVEN. ALTHOUGH I'M PROBABLY DESTINED FOR HELL.

HAROLD DAVIES AND I WERE CHASING THE SAME LADY AND DECIDED TO SETTLE IT WITH A BOXING MATCH. WE FOUGHT LATE AT NIGHT, WHEN THE GYM WAS CLOSED. NOBODY KNEW ABOUT IT EXCEPT US. HAROLD LOADED HIS GLOVES WITH SAND, WHICH DIDN'T JUST MAKE HIS PUNCHES HARDER, IT ALSO GOT INTO MY EYES. WHEN I REFUSED

TO ACCEPT DEFEAT BECAUSE OF THIS, HE BECAME ANGRY. I WOULD NOT LET HIM HAVE JOANNE AND HE THREATENED ME WITH A KNIFE.

THE FOLLOWING SATURDAY I DECIDED WE WOULD REMATCH AND I WAITED FOR HIM NEAR THE CLOSED WANDLE SCHOOL AFTER HE'D BEEN DRINKING. I'D HEARD HE LIKED TO GO AND WATCH THE YOUNGSTERS KISSING BECAUSE THE SCHOOL WAS A POPULAR PLACE FOR THEM TO HANG OUT. THE SCHOOL WAS EMPTY THAT NIGHT SO I CONFRONTED HIM. I WANTED TO FIGHT FOR JOANNE AGAIN. I BROUGHT BOXING GLOVES. BUT HAROLD THREATENED ME WITH THAT KNIFE AGAIN. HE THREATENED TO KILL JOANNE. HE WAS A VIOLENT, HORRIBLE MAN AND I KNEW HE MEANT IT.

I KNOCKED HIM TO THE GROUND WITH A BRICK FROM THE ONES SCATTERED AROUND, AS HE SQUARED UP TO ME. HE FELL BACK AND LAY STILL, BLEEDING, AND I CUT HIS THROAT WITH HIS OWN KNIFE. I WAS STILL ANGRY AND I ALSO PUT SAND IN HIS EYES BECAUSE HIS CHEATING WITH SAND CAUSED ALL THIS.

MY NAME IS JACK MURRAY AND I AM OF SOUND BODY AND MIND. I DO NOT WANT MY DAUGHTER OR MY YOUNG GRANDDAUGHTER TO KNOW ANYTHING ABOUT THIS. IF THE POLICE AND THE NEWSPAPERS CAN KEEP THIS AWAY FROM THEM, I WILL DONATE ALL MY MONEY TO CHARITY.

JACK MURRAY, SEPTEMBER 18TH, 1997

THE END

ACKNOWLEDGEMENTS

They say nobody writes a book alone, and although I was the one who typed all the words, this thing wouldn't be in your hands without the input of some special people. In the order they played a part are: my partner, Jay *'Okay, you can go play on the computer'* Jones, Betsy *'here's a book contract* Reavley, Ian *'I'll edit this into something readable'* Skewis, and Tara *'I'll organise the publication'* Lyons.

Thanks also go to friends and family, for encouragement. And tea. Also, all the other Bloodhound authors, for advice. And for brilliant novels that made me up my game, if only in hope that mine could be half as good as theirs.

www.ingramcontent.com/pod-product-compliance
Lightning Source LLC
Chambersburg PA
CBHW050833190726
48286CB00007B/2070